THE BAGHDAD VILLA

THE BAGHDAD VILLA

Zuheir El-Hetti

translated by Samira Kawar

Interlink Books

An imprint of Interlink Publishing Group, Inc.
Northampton, Massachusetts

First published in 2023 by

Interlink Books
An imprint of Interlink Publishing Group, Inc.
46 Crosby Street
Northampton, Massachusetts 01060
www.interlinkbooks.com

Published in Arabic in 2016 as *Ayyam al-Turab (Days of Dust)*
by Dar Al Tanweer, Tunis, Tunisia

Library of Congress Cataloging-in-Publication Data available
ISBN 978-1-62371-790-2

Printed and bound in the United States of America

Chapter One

HALLUCINATION

Max Ernst: *The Temptation*

Guevara, our mascot in this city of thieves, began barking fiercely at seven last night, prompting me to scold him with a harshness I didn't like to use with him. I hoped to calm him down, but he remained strangely tense and alert, as was his habit when danger in the shape of strangers approached our large, old semi-deserted mansion. No one lived in it anymore, except for my brother Silwan and me. Everyone had left, and death had carried off many of the mansion's former residents. But they had left behind their ghosts, many memories and restless souls.

Prior to the previous evening, Guevara had been afflicted by a kind of inexplicable indolence that came over him sometimes. He was the third generation of dogs bred from one that my grandfather, Ismail Pasha, had brought back with him from Berlin as a puppy, which had been his last ambassadorial post before the Second World War. He was what we call a "wolf dog." His beautiful eyes had a kind of noble, uncomplaining sadness about them. My mother had been very fond of him, and my brother and I had inherited that fondness. He was our only friend in a city in which I couldn't trust a single other inhabitant.

My grandfather had been careful to ensure that his dog, Blondie, only mated with females of the same breed to ensure that the pedigree would remain pure. He had been a strong believer in that principle, exactly like the rest of our upper class, which would not allow any of its members to marry into a family that lacked an ancient lineage or history. I had failed to find an appropriate match for Guevara, so it seemed that his fate had become closely tied to the fate of our family, which was also on the brink of extinction.

When he sensed danger around us, the sad noble look in his eyes would give way to a fierceness that turned him into a frightening creature, even to me. But we had a close relationship with him, which we needed at a time when people with whom we had nothing in common had free rein over the city.

Ever since the occupants of the royal al-Zuhour palace had been dragged through the streets, we had become accustomed to being targeted by waves of intimidation "through legal channels." Many thieves in the regimes that had successively ruled the country had tried to take possession of our spacious mansion, located in a large green area covering one thousand square kilometers. Its grounds contained rows of lemon, orange and palm trees that produce a rare type of dates, and exotic flowers that my grandmother, Mariam, had brought back from Latin America and Asia, and that were unique to Iraq. The building itself dated back to the late nineteenth century. Its construction had been overseen by the British architect Brian

Cooper before he built the royal cemetery in Adhamiyah. It was a unique building, combining Western and Eastern styles with an amazing harmony created by the architect, who had been in love with the East.

The problems we had faced had taken various shapes. Sometimes they had been dressed up as financial incentives. At other times, they had materialized as clear threats, or even as attempts to overwhelm us with bureaucratic difficulties through the state's various departments. All those cheap methods had failed to uproot us from our historic abode, which, as time passed, had become a landmark amid the rapidly expanding neighborhood. As large buildings had replaced the mansions and detached houses, a location would be described as "behind the Pasha's large mansion," or "two turnings after it" and so forth.

My father had dealt with the problems that had come our way, using his remaining influence, connections, and energy, all of which had begun to run out as the shocks kept coming. A small minority of the city's inhabitants had continued to harbor an affection and respect for the "aristocratic class" or "the king's courtiers" as we had been called after the bloody military coup in which the young king, his family and some of his government officials had been dragged through the streets, giving the city a lasting image of barbarity. I couldn't figure out if labeling us like that was a way of getting back at us, or of despising us, or some other evil motive. Actually, I had never had an interest in investigating the ideas of riffraff, or in finding any logic in their extreme actions. I simply had become used to sensing the words directed at me to ascertain the degree of spite or hatred inherent in them.

After my father's death, my mother had taken over the mission of defending "the last bastion of civilization," as she would say when referring to our mansion and the history of our high-born Baghdadi family, which traced itself back to the second Abbasid era. Ultimately, we had survived, and our detractors had disappeared without achieving anything.

But following the occupation, its rotten smell continued to assail my nostrils, and the means used to threaten us had changed completely. It was enough for someone to send someone an envelope containing a bullet and a number specifying how many days one had to leave one's home, failing which physical liquidation would be the alternative. Words were no longer important or necessary to express such an intention in a city inhabited by illiterates, where death glorified its ultimate control in several ways. The city conferred legitimacy on no one after the royals had been dragged through the streets. Everyone had been allowed to participate in shaping the map of bloody chaos in the hope that the people would get voluntary amnesia. As for us, the last vestiges of legitimacy, we were the protectors of the boundaries separating civilization from barbarism. To allow perpetual intellectual darkness to reign, everyone had to collude to cleanse the city of the families and dynasties that did not surrender to the herd mentality's flimsy thought patterns and behavior. So, they decided to get rid of us once and for all.

At exactly seven o'clock yesterday evening, when Guevara began barking loudly, I got a sudden feeling that something was about to happen. But tragic or sudden events were no surprise during such times, when anything could be expected.

That morning, when the housekeeper, Mamluka, came to

see me, I noticed a panicked expression on her face, which I was used to reading. She said nothing and was carrying an envelope with the tips of her right-hand fingers with obvious disgust, as though it contained a dead mouse. Her fitful breathing was almost in step with her careful strides as she approached me slowly in a manner that foreshadowed some nasty event, as though in a Hitchcock film.

Mamluka has been in charge of caring for us since our childhood, so I knew her well. She didn't speak much, and if she did, it was about something important. This tendency had become even more pronounced since my mother's death. She had become even quieter, and her eyes had an expression of chronic anxiety. She had taken on more authority in matters pertaining to our daily lives, as though she wanted to compensate us for the loss of our parents, and she was more protective of Silwan, and was always willing to do anything we asked of her.

But she had started to change recently. Sometimes, while she was cooking for us in the kitchen and avidly smoking her roll-up cigarettes in her usual way, she muttered to herself letting loose curses that spread here and there, just like the bombs that had been dropped over the city. She cursed certain people about whom we knew nothing, using the ugliest of words. They made us laugh, because although we knew those words, we weren't in the habit of using them. Our conversations were different— elegant, devoid of mistakes and rude words, and unrelated to the language of others. We kept them pure to preserve our uniqueness, and we used them as a shield to protect us from the vulgarity surrounding us. Our language was our secret code that allowed us to identify one another, we who belonged to the vanishing class. We had been brought up according to strict rules of speech and behavior. The use of words that breached the limits of politeness and respect was prohibited. We had carefully preserved that strict moral linguistic code, which we shared with our few gradually vanishing acquaintances and relatives, fearing that its demise would signal the loss of our identity. After the first military coup, and the more barbaric ones that followed, many of our acquaintances emigrated or died, and our ethical-linguistic circle shrank. Once the occupation had completed our humiliation, the circle shrank further, finally becoming confined to our remaining family members.

When we would leave the mansion and were forced to mix with others, we would hear a different language that included many obscenities and improper words. I had always been astonished by how other people could let such dirty words roll off their tongues without feeling guilty or cheap, or even embarrassed. Hearing them would make me uncomfortable, as though dirt were sticking to me, trying to turn me into one of them. But as soon as I got back to the mansion and was amongst my select group of people, with all of us using refined language, I would feel clean. We rarely heard such language on the streets, and people would address one another in language devoid of any respect.

Our language gave us clear-cut demographic boundaries. The ancient city that we had built and lived in for seven generations was playing a game of deceitful mirage with us, giving us an identity that we thought was firmly established, but which was not. The country folk, whose numbers were rising in the city, saw us as a minority they must get rid of, leaving nothing to remind them that they were upstarts. It seemed that the obsessive and diligent path we had chosen to follow had earned us inexplicable hostility, making us easy targets in an unbearably hostile environment.

My father had been the one most saddened and affected by the demographic change, especially when someone would address him by his first name, or in the second person, "you." He considered that form of address as equivalent to inflicting physical harm. I had only ever heard him addressing a stranger in the plural, and with utmost respect, regardless of that person's status or family connections. Although he was friendly, he was strict about preserving distances between people, and he believed that humankind starts to decline when the language people use to communicate with one another declines. For humans to progress, and for people to become human, they must acquire knowledge and habits, and cultivate feelings other than those that nature bestows upon all its creatures, otherwise they become vessels that contain life but do not become fully human.

My father had also believed our presence in the city would be ended by events more treacherous than those that had caused the death of the inhabitants of the royal al-Zuhour palace—events that would spare nothing, and that would be even more tragic. He had never imagined that we would go extinct with a whimper, rather than with the loud shouting that he had expected. The human perfection that we had been trying to build within our dynasty for seven generations had collapsed in a frightening way, and it was my bad luck to be the last witness to such an ending, which I realized was not far off.

Mamluka approached and handed me the envelope. A trembling smile that I could not suppress hovered on my lips. I was sure that a terrible evil was approaching, a tragedy that Guevara's barking had foretold. As soon as she handed me the envelope, I felt its heaviness. My fingers curled around a hard object within it, and I immediately guessed its contents. I opened it and brought out a copper-colored bullet with a red line running around its tip, or the part of it that kills. It was wrapped in a piece of lined paper that had been hurriedly torn out of some school copybook, and it simply bore the number 7. It was a chilling omen, immediately confronting me with the dilemma of a death for which I was not prepared.

Mamluka and I stared at each other for a while, frozen by impotence. We communicated with looks rather than words. We were tongue-tied by a bitter surprise that cast an aura around us, making it difficult for us to utter the right words. Anything said would have further complicated matters. Even our breaths seemed to intensify the atmosphere of ominous shock. The killers' message was clear and could not be misconstrued: only two choices. Departure or physical liquidation.

I became aware that Mamluka was still standing before me, expecting some sort of response. I smiled at her with as much politeness as I could muster, and asked her about breakfast. She threw her head back as though to avoid an insult. But in her usual manner, she made no comment, quickly heading for the kitchen to prepare breakfast for us—my brother Silwan and me.

I felt a pleasant numbness as I sat on the terrace overlooking the garden. It had become neglected and the rare flowers that the previous generations had cultivated had disappeared, because economic circumstances had forced me to cut the number of gardeners to one—Mamluka's husband Jawad. Sometimes, my brother Silwan worked in the garden. The materials needed to keep it blooming were no longer available. I had never imagined that the approach of death could give one a strange longing for rest. The longing kept fear at bay, or postponed it, so I felt none.

My first thought was for Silwan. A turbulent, uncontrollable anxiety welled up within me about my brother's fate, and huge questions occurred to me. He was my weak point, and I had never thought that I would be in charge of him, but that was exactly what had happened, after he had lost his mind in the faraway south, along the country's painful Golgotha, or what had become known as "the Highway of Death." He had come up with that name in his repeated delirious ravings after returning to us by a miracle of which we knew nothing. He had been a soldier in an army that had been epically crushed in the battle to free the oil-rich desert. He came back to us, but did not return, because he had left his mind there, on the road between Basra and Nasiriya. He came back filled with horrifying nightmares, leaving behind all that was human. Then he began to endlessly narrate what he had experienced and seen on that accursed road, like an endless black waterfall.

The bullet was still on the glass table by the crystal vase of damask roses. They were of different colors and sizes, and I had picked them in the garden two days before. They had started to wilt. A small transistor radio near the vase emitted a discordant female voice, and with every sentence I picked out linguistic mistakes. Next to it was a tidy pile of white paper, with my father's Parker fountain pen lying on top of it. I made a habit of using it and filling it up with ink every now and then to keep it from drying out, as though I were awaiting my father's return, despite my firm belief that the dead do not come back. Beside it was a patterned metal tray with eight colored glasses on it that we once brought back from the Khan al-Khalili souk in Cairo. I surveyed all this and was seized by a revulsion so strong that it was enough to drown this whole sinister city and all its inhabitants.

I wondered where the courage lay in intimidating a woman living alone with her deranged brother and threatening them with physical liquidation. Gangs of those aspiring to be men were hiding behind that cowardly bullet. They did not speak our select language, and were cowards and liars, who talked incessantly about building, but only knew the language of destruction. Would it not have been worthier of them to have come and threatened me to my face?

When a city, any city, is devoid of real heroes, it becomes a playground for liars who speak gibberish about making history. That is the way Baghdad had become, ever since its legitimacy had been slain on its asphalt streets. Now, it seemed like nothing more than a stagnant pond. That was why people were not ashamed of what they were doing against it, its history, and its people. We and the city were living without any real heroes. It was ruled by pretenders. It was a huge travesty with nightmarishly terrifying creatures that wanted to return us to the days of the apes.

Mamluka served us our breakfast: hard-boiled eggs, two kinds of cheese, a fresh salad and hot milk and tea. We ate it in silence.

Ever since Silwan's return from that strange journey, known

as compulsory military service, he had insisted on only wearing white shirts that all looked the same. A white shirt every day, the same bright, glaring white. He couldn't wear colored clothes anymore, and resolutely rejected anything that wasn't white. Was his insistence a way of searching for the purity that he had lost there? Was he dreaming of regaining it? Why did he insist on buttoning up his collar and cuffs both during the day and at night however hot it was? Why did he go to bed in white clothes, and change into other white clothes when he got up? Was he trying to stop something that the white clothes would show up from entering his body? He had returned from there with many puzzling ways that had never been part of his habits before he had gone on his journey of military service and insanity. He had left behind his innocence, his wishes, his desires, his aspirations, and returned to us in puzzling neutral white.

He didn't utter a word as we ate. A strange smile appeared on his face, which displayed a mixture of bygone good looks and signs of insanity. I had become used to that kind of smile, which I called "the gateway to hallucination." He kept throwing me timid glances, waiting for a suitable opportunity. Whenever he sensed one, he would start narrating the details of his unending nightmares. I had become well-practiced at this psychological game, and I knew how to elude it. Although I felt sorry for him, because talking about his nightmare gave him a sense of relief, I couldn't listen to him every day. The details he liked to delve into depressed me and left me feeling broken. I left the table in a hurry and headed for the large sitting room that was used for receiving guests who no longer visited. It had become deserted, like everything else in the mansion, in which we led a mostly silent existence. Or perhaps it was the mansion that was alive, not us!

Where had the people who had once filled the garden and the mansion's rooms gone? I surveyed the garden, and the trees, which were being consumed by drought. I saw the shadows of those who filled my memory, which was also wilting and drying up. Where had they gone? Since the occupation of the city and the explosion of bind violence, the vacuum had expanded and threatened to swallow us.

The reception room was very large and was divided in two by a row of columns painted in the colors of the light spectrum. There were nine columns, and each was a different color. The larger section was a guest sitting room, and the smaller section was a dining room. The large sitting room could take more than one hundred guests. In the past, which seemed to me like ancient times, my grandfather Ismail, who loved social evenings and holding parties, had almost lived in that room. He had not liked to sit in the library, because he was extremely protective of its contents. They included hundreds of books and manuscripts that had been collected by generations of ancestors and a special section for unfinished manuscripts and rare books that had been bound in a special way to preserve them. Each heir had been careful to add something to the library and to preserve it. Now, it was my turn!

I looked at the big radio lying beneath a white sheet. I surveyed it fearfully, seeing in it evidence of the ruination that had befallen us. I saw how the shine of its mahogany and ivory buttons had dulled, and an image appeared before me of my grandfather surrounded by a group of his close friends, whom he used to invite on the first Thursday of every month to a banquet, followed by a worshipful silence as they listened to the concerts of the great lady singer Umm Kulthoum. Her concerts used to be broadcast live by Sawt al-Arab radio station in Cairo. They used to call her "the lady" as a token of respect. No one just used her name. Those evenings were a ritual that could not be altered once that radio had entered the mansion.

The men sat in the larger part of the room smoking, the cigarette smoke forming a gray cloud with light bluish edges over their heads. Sometimes I can still see it and smell it. They drank vintage Scottish whiskey, although some of them preferred local arak. They responded to the lady's "ahs" with their own "ahs" and tolerated her songs in praise of Gamal Abdel Nasser and his revolutionary command council that had overthrown the monarchy. They were all staunch monarchists, but none of them wanted to spoil the enjoyment of listening to the lady with the beautiful voice, who had contributed to forming a new Arab identity that stretched from the shores of the Atlantic to the Arabian Sea, and even further!

The women worked diligently to prepare delicious dishes of food, then placing them elegantly on the large table made of dark ebony wood at the other side of the room. They eavesdropped through the nine colored columns wearing sly, contented feminine smiles.

I studied the colors of the columns. They had faded, and everyone had departed to the land of no return. But the "ahs" and the aroma of the food and the gray-bluish cloud of smoke hung in the air of the sitting room. I was the only one to enjoy recollecting those moments, and the company of those ghosts that discussed science, art and philosophy.

We were children, and we used to sneak into the drawing room. Entering it was prohibited in order to protect its expensive furniture. My grandfather Ismail and grandmother Mariam had chosen the furniture down to the minutest detail. They had impeccable taste, and their sense of beauty had been polished by their travels, since my grandfather had been an ambassador and representative of the king. He had also been one of the first to help establish the state. Actually, it was not just ordinary furniture. It was an accumulation of details, memories and history that could only be read by those baptized in the secrets of that old mansion. I liked to decipher things so that they seemed like a novel full of nostalgia and wonderful details, and I knew each of its sentences and commas.

Members of our family had inherited a mysterious feeling that was difficult to comprehend! We felt that we were the bearers of a message that we must struggle to deliver. One of its most important hallmarks was civilization, strengthening the values of beauty, sincerity and refinement. As for the recipient of that message, that was a mystery! None of us knew the answer. But that belief had persisted and given us a feeling of superiority, happiness and pride although it seemed to me our message would be received by no one!

Besides the beautiful memories, the rich discussions about science and philosophy, the voice of the lady that drew joyous images and worlds on the walls and never departed, something else attracted me to that room. It was the seven paintings hanging on the walls of the sitting room side of it. My grandfather had bought them during his travels, and they were the focus of thorny discussions about the value and meaning of art. It's likely that those paintings influenced my choice to pursue my higher studies in art.

After receiving that threatening letter, I started to worry about the paintings. Removing them and putting them somewhere else was not something I was willing to consider at all. The radio, the library, the furniture and those paintings above all else were fixtures in the mansion's reception room. I felt that they belonged there forever. They were one of the focal points of the mansion's life, and if they were to be removed, the mansion would die, and if it were to die, they would die with it. So I decided to write this tale, because I believe that writing is an act of survival during a time of ugliness. That was exactly what I wanted to do, to fortify myself against the approaching fear whose faraway footsteps I could hear steadily drawing closer. I wanted to keep myself occupied to ward off the sound of those footsteps and to escape Mamluka's frightened looks. She would usually go into the kitchen and would only come out to perform an important task. But that day, she kept popping up in front of me every now and then, full of urgent questions that she expected me to answer—as though I knew what I ought to do!

The seven paintings were distributed around the walls in beautiful harmony. Together, they inspired a meditative sorrow that I hadn't experienced before. It felt as sharp as a knife blade, unleashing in me a feeling of complete impotence and helplessness in the face of the ruinous storm that was invading anything beautiful that had survived in the city.

Why these paintings in particular, and why these thorny subjects that they evoked?

People usually display uncontroversial paintings on their walls that do not provoke their fears about worrisome existential questions, and do not give rise to philosophical issues. Did my grandfather feel comfortable sitting there with his guests, looking at Böcklin's *Island of the Dead* or watching Max Ernst's strange creatures as they tried to devour Saint Anthony? Or was he thinking of Salome as Caravaggio had imagined her, helping her father to slaughter the prophet John, who seems to be giving in to this fate as he lies on the floor soaked in his blood, while she carries the basket in which she will place his head before performing history's most famous dance?

Where was the logic in my grandfather's choices?

It had never occurred to me or to any of my siblings to ask such questions. No one recalled when those paintings had been hung on the walls. They had always been there, and as time went by, they had become part of our lives, which had passed beneath their gold-plated frames, and they had left their imprint on our memories and cultural identity. As for the secret and the taste considerations that had informed the choice of those paintings, they had gone to the grave with those who had chosen them. Had my grandfather chosen them, or had his wife, my grandmother? Why these ones in particular? Had they discussed them before buying them and bringing them here from faraway places to hang on Baghdadi walls?

All those of whom I could ask such questions were gone, and perhaps it was no longer important to seek the answers. What mattered to me was that I still derived a feeling of comfort and familiarity when I sat amongst them, and I knew that their presence in my life had motivated me to choose fine arts, and plastic arts in particular, as my field of academic study, despite my mother's objections. She hadn't viewed my field of specialization as worthy of our family's history, which had spawned many doctors, diplomats, advisers and other legal and engineering specialists. But our men had avoided the military establishment after it had become sullied with innocent royal blood.

Everyone acknowledged that I had a talent for identifying beauty in paintings and other objects. That talent had facilitated my work as an advisor at the Saddam Center for Arts, which had later fallen victim to the mob's axes, as they attacked it on the pretext of obliterating the name! My mother was the only one who considered my job as a social comedown for our family. She even viewed my having a job as inappropriate, because she believed that a woman must devote herself to bringing up the next generation to preserve family values, and that every woman must be, as she herself had been in her own life, a custodian of the traditions and mores of our disappearing class. When I chose to work, we were not financially in need. What we had managed to hold onto after the nationalizations carried out by successive primitive governments was more than enough to meet our needs. But I had wanted to work in the arts, possibly out of a deep-rooted desire to go against my mother and her views. Her sick temperament swung between irritation and complaint. Her words had always included obscure or coded connotations that had not been easy for me to detect, at least not immediately.

My study of the plastic arts had given me the ability to withstand the cruel desertification of reality, and to dance freely on the mountain tops in my daydreams. But at that moment, I felt that I was the only remaining link in the mansion's history, and the reception room gave me the sense of security that I needed.

Had I opened the door, I might have found Mamluka standing behind it, trying to eavesdrop on me to find out if I was crying. I hadn't cried for a long time. I couldn't remember the last time I had cried. Actually, I didn't want to remember.

Since receiving that envelope, I felt Mamluka eyes watching me keenly. I saw her all the time, moving around for no reason, and every time she passed me, she threw me an inquiring look.

I wasn't in the mood to talk about what the envelope meant. We both knew. I didn't want to think of the next steps, least of all then. My attention was focused on writing.

As for why and for whom I was writing, I had no idea. Did I want to record the tragic end of our family? Why? Would anyone care? I hardly knew anyone in the city, which had become so ruralized that it could no longer be called a city, save for the size of its inhabitants, who massed together so closely it was difficult to penetrate them. Our real friends and acquaintances had fled, emigrated, or died. There was no one. But I still wanted to write. I wanted to confront present fear with memories of the past. I wondered why the past was always more beautiful than the present.

In the distant past, our neighborhood had been the most refined and oldest quarter in the capital, but it had changed with the speed of a flood that rushes forward with a roar. The entire city had changed. My mother had been in the habit of saying that we had known the neighbors at one time. Now we didn't know who lived next door. Actually, they knew us, and they knew one another, and they regarded us as though we were the strangers. I was besieged by hostile glances whenever I left the mansion or returned to it. They were part of a different world, whose maps were unknown to us. According to Mamluka, they called us all sorts of names intended to undermine our status. The Bataween district had turned into an area bustling with commercial activity day and night. Its beautiful old buildings, like our mansion, were nostalgic evidence that clearly indicated a bygone golden age and a miserable present.

Once, a fellow student at university who had lived in the same neighborhood told me that I was "aristocratic." She had made it sound like an accusation that I should be ashamed of. That kind of babble had originated in the middle of the previous century, when some illiterates had borrowed some words from the global communist dictionary and generalized them without any real understanding of their serious social connotations. They had directed them like fireballs against the likes of ourselves. My father had once said to me, "Iraq was able to establish the largest communist party in the Middle East, but none of its members had read Marx's *Kapital* for the simple reason that it had not been translated into Arabic at the time. Only excerpts from it were translated in a rudimentary and inaccurate manner, which is why the biggest illiterate Communist Party in the world had been established here."

Waves of hatred had targeted families with an ancient history as the rule of illiterates and pseudo intellectuals had continued. Coups had come in waves, and we were tossed from one to the next as weightless as a feather, unable to integrate. Legitimacy had turned into a parasitic body, a secret sect. Those carrying out coups were after power, and their aim was to blend us into their cheap mix, and to teach us how to adapt to hostile environments. Many of us had weakened and fallen along the painful path. It would have been easy for us to immigrate. My sister Rabab had been the most eager family champion of that idea and had suggested it to my father every now and then. But he had firmly refused, reminding us that we were living in the land of our forefathers, and that we could not abandon it for the sake of a bunch of upstarts who had forcibly seized power. After such a decisive pronouncement, we would lower our heads and an air of disappointment would settle over us that would also affect my father himself. But I no longer doubted that when death had taken him by surprise he had begun to consider immigrating just as we had—because the problem had been much deeper and much more pervasive than "a bunch of upstarts."

No one could live virtuously and according to higher principles amid such moral chaos. We all knew that things in this city had reached the lowest possible level, and that there was no hope of a miracle that would save us. We were people who belonged to a "beautiful bygone time" that everyone else wanted to shovel earth over and bury.

The seven paintings hanging on the sitting room walls in an attractive and suggestive way greatly affected my mood, and perhaps even shaped it. There I was, perhaps under the influence of what had happened, choosing to spend my time, which was running out, in that hall, writing and surveying those paintings, which had connotations relevant to how our family situation had developed.

That day, I sat before Max Ernst's painting *The Temptation of Saint Anthony*. It showed the saint wrapped in a red robe, surrounded on all sides by hellish creatures of different shapes and sizes, trying to tear him apart, to grab the very last flame of faith within him and extinguish his life. He appears to both resist and surrender simultaneously. The artist has abandoned him to his fate, unsure. Anyone who contemplates this painting will be forced to think about the duality of good and evil and the long bloody conflict between them, the ever-lasting battle that began with Cain and Abel and which continued as I wrote my memoir, my story, my will, or anything else that my writing could be called. Those same ugly creatures were outside the mansion, tearing up each other, and I asked in despair, "What have I to do with all that filth?"

Early on, I had been scared to look at that painting for long. But I had learned to view it from a different perspective. I had started to see hope in it, a renewal of hope, or a renewal of illusion, the victory of the virtuous will and the defeat of absolute evil—who knows?

But now I realized that no matter how much I might look away from the ugliness surrounding me, it was present then and there, behind me, under me and around me. And I realized it was trying to swallow me up, although I liked to cling to hope, even if it was an illusion.

Every first Thursday of the month, we were in the habit of giving the mansion a full spring cleaning. The entire family would get together, but things weren't the way they used to be. The number of people working at the mansion had dwindled, and only Mamluka remained. She had grown too old to clean all the mansion's eighteen rooms, in addition to the reception rooms and the library, even with help from her niece, whose name I can't remember. We were also used to cooking distinctive and special dishes that day, burning sticks of Omani incense and sprinkling water on all the windows so that the fragrance would spread. We would cut flowers, fill the vases, dress up and wear perfume—not for anyone in particular, but for ourselves, our memories, our traditions, and the past that we inhabited more than the present. We would celebrate ourselves, delude ourselves, if only for one evening, that we were still the masters of this city, which had lost its sanity. We would call it the day of "acceptance" and bring together remaining loved ones.

On that day, my sisters Rabab and Balqis would come with their children and husbands. We would all indulge in the luxury of complaining about economic, political, social, and religious conditions. Nothing in that miserable city was to our taste. Rabab and Balqis would arrive a few hours before their husbands and children. After the three of us had prepared the food and laid the table, we would sit in the smaller reception room rather than here in the larger sitting room. We had stopped gathering in the sitting room since our mother died. Perhaps we were trying to outwit grief by avoiding spots that were full of memories.

Before the meal, Silwan would try to repeat parts of his never-ending nightmares, which had caused him to swing between reason and insanity. He had been sentenced to remain in that grey area for ever, as the family doctor had told us before immigrating to Scotland.

Silwan was unable to comprehend the horrors he had experienced on the "Highway of Death". As far as he was concerned, nothing had ended. Sometimes, I wondered if those horrors had ended for us, for me. I had no definite answer. He was unable to take the nightmare to its absolute darkest limit, so he had remained in the land of absolute insanity.

He continued to torture us as he tried to tell us with genuine honesty and emotion that the cats there ate corpses and spoke, and that stray dogs bit heads and limbs. As for the hyenas, they searched among the gravely injured soldiers because, as the hyenas "told him," they enjoyed snatching away what little remained of those lives.

We would all surely try, in different ways ranging from being kind to scolding him, to persuade him to postpone relating his nightmare until after the meal. The poor fellow would fall reluctantly silent, and his sorrow would kill our last hope of forgetting our misery. Repeating his tale gave him some relief from mental pressures, so he would find a way in the end to start telling it all over again. He did this every day, and when we all avoided him, including Mamluka, he would sit beside Guevara and speak to him seriously. What mattered was to find someone who would listen to him, even a dog with sad and beautiful eyes for whom we could find no female worthy of his pedigree. The details in his story increased or decreased according to how restless his listener became. He didn't look straight into the eyes of whoever he was speaking to, his gaze escaping to where it could not be captured. Was Silwan afraid we would accuse him of being mad, or of lying or exaggerating? Or did he want to avoid seeing our weariness of his black unending dream?

After coming back to us in such a condition, his speech became uncharacteristically rapid. A white froth would gather at the edges of his mouth, but he would be oblivious to it. He would not even stop to catch his breath and would keep talking until I thought he would choke on the words pouring out of his mouth. Where his torrent of words came from was beyond me. He would stretch his neck forward and upward, his veins protruding unattractively, and would look frightening, as though he were someone else, not the brother I knew. He would knot the fingers of both his hands together in his lap as though one hand wanted to break the fingers of the other. The wall holding back his words would collapse, and he would lose the ability to stop. He would repeat things on an on indefinitely, so that looking at his face required a courage that I had begun to lose.

The only thing that limited the flow of his hallucinations was a method he had discovered himself: house cleaning! At first, I was embarrassed and even ashamed that he was sharing Mamluka's cleaning chores. I tried to stop him, but I discovered that hard physical work consumed his energy and reduced the strength of his hallucinations. It calmed him down and made him less talkative. He discharged his madness and anger by polishing the furniture till it shone, washing the floors, and pruning the trees. While performing these chores, he muttered to himself as though speaking in a language I didn't know. He always ensured that Guevara was nearby. When night fell, he would sleep like a child in his white buttoned shirt, always in the same position—on his back, without turning to the right or the left. Sometimes, I would sneak into his room to check on him and would be overwhelmed with sadness, because he looked like someone who was preparing for death in that unchanging position.

All those years, I had tried to communicate with him visually when he spoke to me, which he did often. But he was good at escaping to where I could not reach him. I felt impotent, disappointed, and frustrated that the only thing I could do was listen to his ravings while I thought of other things. I felt angry that he had lost his mind in a trivial war that had been managed by people with sick mentalities. All wars are trivial, and it's unfair that one must pay the price of the stupidity and triviality of others.

My goodness, he had been so handsome before the war, exuding brilliance, liveliness, and intelligence. He had been so elegant and charming, a dream catch for young women of refined families, both in this city or abroad, where the young girls of immigrant families waited. Each of them might have agreed to lose her fingers just to get close to him. But now! My god, how was I to regain Silwan so that he would at least bear the burden of the looming ending instead of me?

Sometimes, like shadows secretly plucked from the land of insanity, the human expressions he had lost would re-emerge, and I would see the brother Silwan that I knew, like someone coming through a thick fog. I had no idea how or when I could clutch that brilliant split second. The last time it had occurred had been a few days before, when we were eating the vegetable soup that he liked. Perhaps that was because he had been the one to cultivate those vegetables in the garden. For a moment after the first mouthful, he had closed his eyes, and a smile that came from afar and that I recognized had appeared. He seemed content, the aggressive looks that had taken over his features were gone and his lost good looks had returned. His charming smile, which had pleased us so much because he was the only brother to us four sisters, was wider. Those few seconds made me hold on to a hope that was weaker than the threads of a spiderweb. I wondered if insanity had been unable to conquer him completely. There was something deep inside him that continued to resist. I didn't know what it was, but he was resisting.

The nightmare of hallucination seemed like ugly abscesses that emerged and grew in his brain until his ability to resist collapsed, and his only choice was to spew out the nightmare. At that point, it didn't matter who was listening to him. It could be me, Mamluka, the dog, Guevara, or even the parrot, Pavarotti. Then he would feel some relief, although I knew that it was simply a truce, because his battle with nightmares was unending, just like Sisyphus with the rock. Was this some sort of divine punishment? But what had Silwan done to deserve a punishment like that of Sisyphus, who challenged the gods?

I had never thought of listening to his frightening nightmare till the end. I could not. Was it his imagination that was producing all that purulence? What sort of imagination was capable of producing such a vast quantity of turbulent hallucination?

After I finished writing those lines, I lifted my gaze like someone who had received a mysterious call, and I re-examined Max Ernst's painting.

How was the artist able to embody all those ugly, frightening creatures in his painting? Where did they come from? Did he also suffer hallucinations like Silwan? Or perhaps it was because he was a Jew who had escaped the Holocaust? Did he really survive, or did the evil of the murderers' and their ghosts keep chasing him until his death? Could Silwan in the end get rid of all these frightening creatures that wanted to send him to hell, as the hero of the painting Saint Anthony did, or would they conquer him? Although my brother was not a saint, I kept comparing the two of them and held on to the hope that he would survive the death trap that had been set for him.

Then I decided that, for once, I would hear out his hallucinations till the end. There was no need for me to look for him or call him. He would approach me anyway, once Guevara tired of listening to him and got up, wagging his tail with boredom and ignoring Silwan's pleas to remain with him like a faithful listener.

As soon as Guevara moved away, I heard Silwan's slow, hesitant footsteps. He gave a hesitant knock and walked in before hearing my voice. He sat before me calmly, gave me a questioning, smiling anxious look as though he were asking me if I were willing to listen to him. As soon as I smiled back, the muscles of his mouth moved energetically to spew out a flood of the hallucinations that his doctor—who had also emigrated—had told us would be with him for good.

I decided to write down everything. The threat I had received awakened chaotic feelings within me and I wanted to record them for some obscure reason—perhaps to relieve the pressure that the fear of the threat was exerting on me, or because I was the last in a family line that was disappearing, or perhaps because my grandmother Mariam began her memoirs—which I read after her death—by saying, "I want to write to feel liberated." She did not say whom she wanted to be liberated from, but it was reassuring to walk in her footsteps.

How can I write our history? How can I feel liberated without mentioning Silwan's nightmares, which have in the end become our nightmares, even though we did not travel along the "highway of death"?

As soon as he saw me, he sensed I was in a mood that would allow him to talk. His smile widened, and the right corner of his mouth drooped strangely. There was something different about his smile. My heart beat faster in the hope that there was some change in the details to which I had become accustomed, or that the spark of life that had been swallowed up by the darkness could be revived. Or was he contemptuous of me? Of us, because we weren't up to accepting the truth in which he believed and which he had brought back from "there"?

I didn't utter a word. I met his erratic gaze, giving him a welcoming smile that suggested that I was fully willing to listen to anything he wanted to say until he was ready to stop. My willingness was matched by his readiness to tell his story without repeating the unintelligible tales that he had often related as though they were images in his mind that others didn't need to understand.

His mouth regained its handsome shape, and the smile was replaced by a serious look that I hadn't seen on his face for some time.

"Do you know that during war, the dread of death is replaced by an intense calm, a calm that reconciles us to death, and even makes us wish for it as the only salvation as it approaches? It banishes our shadows and becomes the shadow! It's here, among us, within us. We see it among the shrapnel and missiles. We hear its screaming mingling with the sound of aircraft. Our reactive and irrational movements indicate that it's approaching. We see glimpses of it in the thoughts of a comrade in arms who begins to pray in surrender or pleading. We draw closer, and it seems careless, erasing our dreams that are scattered throughout the spaces that stretch between the homes we've come from and the desert in which we'll die, and it gives us the dream of desiring salvation!

"Over there, I used to scream in a strange way that even frightened me. It wasn't screaming, it was the bark of an animal that resides deep within us. We can call it pure panic that is devoid of any human aspect. If I wanted to reproduce those sounds, I wouldn't be able to, although I can still hear them. It was a scream that could only be made by a creature at that moment, a moment that doesn't come again unless a deeply rooted animalism from within us is called up.

"The dying soldier not far from me was trying to resist in vain as he saw the brown hyenas with black spots drawing closer to his neck. Their rotten smell preceded them. He was resisting with strange, instinctive movements, despite his bleeding wound, because those creatures, which usually eat corpses, had changed their habits. They no longer approached dead bodies, which were all over the place in that desert. They started searching for those who were still barely alive, enhancing their enjoyment by killing before consuming.

"The poor soldier was reduced to nothing more than bulging eyes. He could no longer bark like me, nor could he ask for help in that desert that stretched into a horizon from which there was no escape except into the sky. Vast areas of nothingness that seemed as though they had been created especially for dying. Whom could he have asked for help, anyway? There was nothing there to stop the approaching hyenas, which weren't frightened of anyone. He looked at me pleadingly, and I recognized a clear wish in his bulging eyes for a quick death. I realized it when his unintelligible instinctive movements ceased. I saw it in his silent pleading eyes, in his features, which seemed calmly certain that I would do the job."

Silwan was silent for a few moments. He shut his eyes, then continued, "I did not hesitate to pick up my weapon, which I had been given to fight an enemy that I didn't know. I shot him, and I shot at the hyenas. Had he not wanted a quick death? I saved him. Or perhaps I killed him out of selfishness. Actually, I not only wanted to fulfill his wish of saving him from being consumed by wild animals while he was still breathing. I wanted to spare myself from seeing such a horrible sight. I wanted to shoot my own destiny. Do you understand me, Ghosnelban? I preempted the hyenas by taking away from him the thing that was exciting their instincts. I confronted them in the hope that they would be scared of me. I gave him the possibility of turning into a martyr. If the animals were to feed on us, we would not be considered martyrs, but if we were killed by a bullet, or by a pilot from Chicago or California, we would instantly become martyrs. Isn't that so, Ghosnelban?"

I awoke from the terror of the scene he had just recounted to the impact of his difficult question. No words left my lips. He noted my confusion and continued, "Do you know that I used to hide behind all of you for protection during those difficult times? I used to conjure up as many memories of all of you as I could, because they gave me a feeling of security. They built a warm, protective wall around me. That weird day turned into an endless time, a time and place outside the parameters of time and place that I knew, and memories were my refuge. They were the only thing that kept the desire for death away from me. I saw death as a comfort, as a salvation from the suffering I was going through for trivial reasons. I was sure that the disappearance of memories at a time like that would mean surrendering to death. So I immersed myself in memories, down to the minutest details, the sweetest and the bitterest. I conjured up those we had lost to death, and I lived with them. I laughed, cried, spoke, shouted, agreed, and disagreed. One thing worried me. I was unable to remember them at our house. They were always somewhere cloudy. So I went back home.

"I had never before known the importance of names, and that they are the first thing that receives a person, and the last thing that remains with that person till the very end. Out of the circle of the name we are known by in our lives emerges the growing circle of memories linked to that name. When a person dies, the name dies and becomes a shadow from the past in the memories of those we know, who gradually die themselves. I wanted to give those memories, which I had collected from the old times, the opportunity to shine for the last time, so that I could see them glowing in the desert sky like a brilliant collection of meteors that would dazzle the sight, to be followed by eternal peace. Memories gave me a feeling that I still existed and was not an accidental event in life. Otherwise, what was the meaning of my existence?

"Strangely, as I reviewed those memories amid the terror of that desert during that hard time, I felt no aggression, no disgust, no embarrassment, no denial, or anything. The approach of death gives us the satisfaction of forgiveness. I felt love for my supine body and wished I would not lose it in the desert. I wished that if I were to die, that I would be eaten to the very last piece by predators and beasts, so that my shredded body would not infringe on the desert's breath-taking beauty and awe-inspiring silence, which we were stupidly deforming. I saw our presence, the animals that tracked us, the burned-out wreckage of our vehicles, the names, and the many corpses as indestructible garbage. I felt that we were in the wrong place, that we had no connection whatsoever to the desert's mysterious beauty. I was sure that the animals, the sun, the wind, the sands and even the silence, would take care of removing us and correcting the mistakes, so that beauty would return to where it belonged, and no trace of us would remain.

"All of us have recorded memories that we dig up, choosing its images with a lovely divine levity. I told myself that everything would ultimately be wiped out, and that each body would perish. I would leave a body divided among the guts of wild animals, scattered body parts separated by distances as though they had never existed. The wind would scatter me in all directions. I hoped that my heart would end up as far north as possible, because the north had always excited me and filled me with longing.

"Fever attacked me in violent waves that wracked my weak body like a feather blown around by a storm kicked up by the horses of ancient gods. Gods that had once basked here in this part of the world that witnessed the birth of everything when the gods lived among their creatures and spoke to them. I was able to feel them, then. Yes, the gods were close to me.

"The pain, the memories, the waves of fever, the hostile climate, the ever-present shadow of death, my acquaintances, my history, my unfulfilled wishes, the gods that had lived there. All that allowed me to gain supernatural powers, or perhaps I was possessed by the soul of a tortured god. I had previously thought that a human being's mind determined his course. How wrong I had been. We are all wrong, Ghosnelban. My senses became so powerful that they, rather than my mind, took control of me. My hearing grew so keen that I thought my ears had grown bigger. My weak sight, which had been a lifelong problem, became very strong. My sense of smell became so acute that I was able to recognize smells and detect the odor of anything drawing close to me even before seeing it. My senses allowed me to hear the sounds of the animals devouring the bodies of our dead. I could hear the crackling of limbs and bones as they were being crushed by their teeth. I lay on my back to enjoy one last look at the blue sky, when all my senses were awakened by a massive cloud of dust that drew my attention and that of all the creatures that were waiting to attack our dead and those of us who were still alive. A large crow not far from me squawked. His black feathers, painted by the oil of the gods, glistened with every move that he made. I had not known before that such unintelligible squawking was a language they used to communicate with one another. I only realized it when I gained the ability to decipher that language. When the crow circled me slowly several times, the way it had done for thousands of years, it said, as though addressing me, 'It's the rats.'"

I got goose bumps as I sank into Silwan's nightmares. I was seized by conflicting feelings: tenderness, pity, and a desire to shout at him to be quiet, because I couldn't t keep listening till the end, which didn't seem to be in sight. But I was writing down what he said. I felt it was my responsibility to do so. We'd all become part of this country's unending nightmare. We moved within it, played our roles, slept, multiplied, prayed, complained, wished for things. But we were in a ditch!

"To be honest, Ghosnelban, despite all the pain I was in, I was in a state closer to joy, because the gods had given me their powers. There I was able to understand the language of the birds, which had remained unintelligible to humankind since the days of Solomon the Great! I wanted to raise my head slightly to ascertain the arrival of the rats and that they were really the cause of that massive cloud of dust. I couldn't. But I saw many cats that had taken up positions on the surfaces of the smashed machines. They moved along them elegantly, crouching and meowing scarily in perturbed anticipation. The cats stared at the large cloud and seemed ready to pounce on the approaching horde of rats that had come from the swamps, rubbish dumps, and neglected cemeteries of nearby cities. An old gray cat meowed distinctively and yelled at the other cats, 'Be careful about doing anything stupid. These aren't like the rats you know and are used to hunting. They're savage beasts that can kill any of us with one bite. Avoid them. They're dirty, savage, and primitive. They move in very large numbers. We don't want to fight a battle that will have an uncertain outcome.' The cats meowed, confirming they had received the orders and that they were willing to fight. I wasn't breathing for fear of attracting the animals' attention.

"Cold seeped into my limbs, which seemed to be turning into marble and kept crawling toward my heart, even though the sweat was running down my brow. I heard a voice similar to a human voice, but it wasn't human. It was coming from a faraway mountain, and it was expanding across the desert. It was Noah, shouting firmly, "The flood is coming, and those who do not believe in it are mistaken." The voice was the echo of the eternal call that Noah had released in these parts thousands of years ago. A call that doesn't dissipate in space and isn't lost in oblivion. It echoed within me: 'the flood, salvation'! The times intermingled in my mind. Had the flood arrived? Was I hearing the vibrations of its thunderous warning sound that had been sounding since the beginning of time? My body continued to shake with relentless fever, and salty sweat kept trickling onto my stiffened lips.

"The rotten smell announced that the hyenas were getting close again. One of them was talking, but the others weren't paying him real attention. He was telling them about the beauty of feasting on bodies that were still alive and the tastiness of fresh warm flesh. I wondered if there were any others still alive besides myself. I wished there had been another comrade beside me who could do me the same favor I had done that soldier. The smell was coming closer and closer. I wished it would get hold of my neck and turn me into a corpse in one bite. They say a hyena's bite can break bones. But no, I would ask him, beg him to start with my neck. The smell got closer. It was a large scary hyena that had narrowed its yellowish eyes, stretched forward its head and opened its mouth to reveal its canines. Another small hyena behind him asked, 'Is he alive or dead?' I replied, 'I'm alive, and I'm your feast and I'm not scared. All I ask for is a quick death, which I crave.' When the large hyena heard my words, he stopped, looked at me, then turned around, and pushed back the smaller hyena.

"I lost consciousness and woke up to a hideous voice that almost tore my ears as it screamed at the hordes that were advancing from the depths of hell, 'He's scared, surround him, I know for sure from the same gift that the Lord gave us to foretell an earthquake and the sinking of ships that this human is scared. Chase him mercilessly. He will resist. Attack him with your teeth, make him bleed. The sight of his own blood will increase his panic.' I heard the savage bark of a still undefeated soldier who was still hoping to survive. It was a blood-curdling, non-human sound. I saw him falling in defeat and meekly receiving the rat bites that can pierce iron. I tried to raise my head to see what was happening exactly, but I didn't have the strength. My head fell back onto the hard ground, and I began to beg the god of rats to take my soul in a more merciful way.

"Hundreds of rats were biting the soldier's body as he moaned, and his resistance ebbed away. Increasing numbers of rats were turning his corpse into nothing more than a skeleton amid a pool of blood that waves of Persian gold-digging ants were starting to occupy. One of them shouted, 'Store as much as you can of the defeated army's flesh.' I wondered 'But where are you, Solomon the Great? What mission have you entrusted to this army of yours?'

"The crow, whose words had been the first that I had understood, said to his friend—whose beak became blood-stained as it consumed a piece of flesh that it tossed upward, quickly and elegantly opening its beak to happily gobble up— 'Damn it, why is our flock so late? Where are the others? They're going to miss the feast.' The other crow answered, 'The dead are everywhere. The whole South has turned into a cemetery.'"

Silwan's facial expressions transported him from one stage of grief to the next. I considered suggesting a truce or anything else to get him to stop that flood of frightening hallucinations. But he was oblivious to any of my moves, and it even seemed that he no longer cared if I was still listening. He no doubt wanted to empty his head of the images that pressured him.

For my part, I wanted to confront him, to tell him that these were hallucinations caused by the fever, imaginings that had come from a place that had preoccupied him. But I was scared that I'd push him away if I did that. I preferred to let him keep going in the hope that his story would get to the point I had sought for a long time without getting an answer from him: "How did you come out of that ordeal, Silwan?"

"The lazy gray cat got up and arched its back as though it were warming up for the approaching battle. It seemed to be expressing its joy at the spectacle of so many cats awaiting his signal to start showing their strength. A massive army of cats as far as the eye could see. The gray cat puffed itself up joyfully as it emitted a sound like the scream of an ugly old lady who kidnapped children to live on their blood. A terrible unified meow by the other cats arose, and the grand parade marched forward behind the gray cat like a row of witches out of hell.

"It was a strange day, but no one wants to believe me. It was a day that doesn't belong to our times but seemed as though it had sprung up from the very ancient past.

"Pain is usually a sign of life. The dead don't feel pain, as you know. So I was pleased about my pain and would start worrying when it became duller, and to wonder about the place where I would go.

"A hyena dragged away a nearby body, and I felt I was moving forward in the queue of death, realizing that in the end, I would be first in line. I remembered when our father would take us to the cattle market that was haphazardly held throughout the city as the feast of the sacrifice, Eid al-Adha, approached. Do you remember, Ghosnelban?"

I didn't respond.

He continued, "The animals that stood in the queue of death knew that they would be slaughtered, and so did we. We considered that they must be slaughtered so that the city would get its fill of blood and its people would satisfy their greed for meat. The animals also knew that they had lost the battle of survival and that they must stand in that line. That is how I felt. But who was it that had organized our queue of death in that beautiful desert?

"We called those 'tame' animals sacrifices. A sacrifice that we offered to wash away our sins. The bigger the sacrificed animal, the more its blood would wash away big sins. Did you know that when the Babylonians were stricken with drought or the plague, or when their existence was threatened by a foreign enemy, they used to make many such sacrificial offerings in quick succession so that the smell of blood would reach the gods inhabiting the highest heavens, and they would respond to the pleadings of their subjects and save them from their dark fate? That is what I thought of when I was there on the "highway of death." I was on the spot where those rituals had been practiced thousands of years ago. We were close to Ur, which is now known by the ugly name of 'Nasiriya.' But it seems that the gods have deserted their old homes, and our blood is no longer of interest to them. Oblivion is our fate, isn't it?"

The words poured out of him as though they'd been trapped for a long time and wanted to break free. He spoke quickly and abnormally, and some of what he said didn't sound like it was being articulated in a human voice. He sounded like an automatic machine with no feelings or sensations. No words were stressed to express their weight or importance. It was a confusing, cruel torrent that lacked humanity. As I wrote down what he was telling me, I was struck by nausea and hesitancy. For the first time, I felt scared of being alone with him in this large reception room, which seemed to me like a museum, or a cemetery dominated by the awe inspired by the seven paintings. Whether our grandfather or grandmother hung them up in this way was unknown to us. Was I really with my brother, whom I'd known since birth, or was I with a stranger who'd come from somewhere I didn't know? As he talked, his eyes staring into the distance, I was assailed by a terrifying question: Who is this person sitting in front of me now?

He continued, "During one of those sacrificial feasts, I was watching a large bull of the kind my father insisted on buying every year. I watched as he was being slaughtered by the butchers. Their eyes flashed with an anger that was inexplicable to me, even though the poor creature had surrendered with the meekness of one who believed in fate and showed no inclination to resist. His large, teary eyes searched for salvation in a world we couldn't see. They recited religious verses quickly with a slovenly boredom, and sometimes they shortened them.

"The bull made two separate noises. One came from his mouth, which had a white froth around it. The other came from his half-cut throat, from which arose the vapor of his hot blood, which spilled onto the road's asphalt, turning it bright red. The signs of barbaric joy appeared on everyone's faces as the bull collapsed in surrender to the rhythm of death."

I was unable to resist the nausea arising within me or to listen any longer I suggested that we postpone the rest of the story until tomorrow. I would wait to ask him the question that nagged at me, about how he had survived.

"The reason that the animals surrounded us there so quickly and strangely from all directions was the smell of spilt blood, the smell of the remains of the defeated army. I had to accept, or more accurately, to surrender to my fate as a sacrifice. I had to become the sacrificial bull. I wasn't objecting. But what made me hesitate every time I was about to surrender was a thought that disturbed me. A sacrifice for what? So that the defeated army would be victorious? How so, when most of my comrades had died as they fled in that desert from hunger, thirst, or the bullets of those barbarians who pursued them because they had fled? The spectacle was strange and abnormal, the alliance between those animals and those who were pursuing us in the desert. Armies came from all over the world to liberate us, and they pursued us and used their terrible machines to kill us and shred our bodies. A leadership that insisted that our death was a victory against the conniving invaders, so we should all die."

I said, "Do you know, Silwan, that you have told all of us these stories several times? But never once have you told us how you survived being killed by animals. You have forced us to reconsider animals—even our faithful dog Guevara has started to make me feel uncomfortable when he looks at me for too long. Questions that I had never thought of before start occurring to me, starting with "What if Guevara had been there?" I mean on the road where the bodies of the defeated army had lain. Would he have taken part in tearing apart those bodies, even though he was our civilized dog? What about our lovely white parrot, Pavarotti, whom our grandmother had brought over from Brazil, and whom Rabab had spent many years teaching the word "*marhaba*," which was the only human word he knew?"

Silwan's eyes were wide open, unblinking, and his expression was one of displeasure at my hints that his story wasn't credible. His silence and looks prompted me to think that he might be right. Sometimes, it's easy for us to bury our heads in the sand and ignore the truth, even when it is staring us in the face. But I was adamant about my question, which he'd always ignored. "Why don't you tell us how you survived? How can I accept your story—which is difficult to believe but which you keep repeating—if you don't tell me who saved you from death, or how you saved yourself when you were unable to move?"

He continued to stare at me, and his expression become reproachful. "The story I repeatedly tell is, to me, the truth that I experienced, and it will remain with me till the very end of my life. But to avoid dragging it out as I tell it to you—I don't know who saved me. I can't remember."

I felt I was close to grasping the end of his nightmare. Perhaps if he were to remember it, or to pluck up the courage to tell it, his hallucinations would end. So I kept pressuring him, although I knew that this made him suffer. "Please, tell me what happened. How did you come out alive?"

Conflicting expressions appeared on his face. He pursed his lips and shut his eyes. I was unable to predict what he might do, but I was fairly sure he wouldn't be angry. In the past, when he used to get angry, I could clearly see it coming. He would clench his teeth, but he wasn't doing that. I couldn't understand his reactions anymore. I said, "I'm writing the story of this house and its inhabitants, including those who're dead. I'm almost able to write it till the end. Rabab and Balqis have other stories in other homes. Only you and I are left. Go on, tell me."

I thought his silence would last a long time, and that in the end he wouldn't say anything. But he suddenly began to speak in a tender, submissive voice.

"The darkness I could see and feel within me grew more intense. Weariness with life reached its full extent, just like the bull that was waiting for its own salvation. Merely remaining alive became a big burden. Actually, it became unbearable torture. The familiar appearance of things started to fade, to become invisible, to slowly disappear—the sky, the ground, the savage creatures, the remains of the broken army, everything. New things I had never seen before began to replace them. I heard beautiful voices singing a tune I'd never heard before— a comforting, numbing tune like a wave of light that washed my tired soul. Processions of ghostly creatures in massive numbers filled the place. I felt their abundant presence, but I couldn't fully make out their appearance. They were of different heights, but they had one thing in common that I can't accurately describe: their bodies. They looked as though they lacked the density of our bodies, and they were permeated by light every now and then. Their voices, their music, their strange beauty, the brilliant light with which they played—they were coming from everywhere and nowhere. I became certain that those creatures were coming toward me, and I began waiting for them with an indescribable eagerness. They must have come to take me with them. I also wanted to play with the light. Those creatures were pulling me, and I resisted surrendering to the savage creatures around me. The ants had begun to dig tunnels beneath my body, which was preparing to become a corpse. The ants didn't expect me to resist. Resistance was futile and a rebellion against fate. If I fell asleep and closed my eyes forever, that would be the signal that would mean one thing only to the waiting creatures: the start of plundering my body, and the end of my resistance. It seemed to me as though those ghostly creatures were fighting over who would take me in the end. The only thing I cared about was ending the pain. My body was the dirt I wanted to get rid of. I was hoping to see Noah before my end, a great giant coming out of the depths of the desert, his head in the sky and his limbs in the sand, carrying a boat on his shoulder and looking for me."

He fell silent, and I couldn't stop my eagerness, which was fueled by my frustration. So I asked, "And then?"

"I don't know. I couldn't comprehend or think. I started having feelings that I had never known existed within me. Their stormy waves tossed me about in the desert glare, feelings that made me glow with the story of my life, feelings living within that life. The decision was no longer mine. I was exhausted, hungry, in pain, powerless. How could I resist? Why would I resist? I surrendered."

"But you came out alive! For God's sake, Silwan, tell me

how you came out alive? Please let me complete the story before you and I are finished off…" I wanted to say "by a bullet," but I kept quiet.

He said, "You want me to end the story according to your own standards. You think stories have happy or sad endings. You measure my words and their accuracy according to the standards of your world, without accepting the existence of another world."

He was silent for a short while, then called over Guevara. I begged him to go on, to tell me, even if it was those creatures that I didn't believe in that had saved him, or even the prophet Noah. I begged him, saying, "Just tell me, after you fell asleep or surrendered, where did you wake up? Where did you find yourself?"

But he kept calling out to Guevara and looking for him, avoiding a confrontation he didn't want. Why did those creatures and speaking animals not kill him? How did he return from that land of futility in such a state of insanity and hallucination? I knew it was cruel of me to ask such questions, but hadn't we been silently asking them to ourselves ever since he came back from there? Wouldn't his death have been a more merciful salvation than this incomplete return? The words flashed like the blade of a knife in the dark. His death. Our salvation!

I tried to get up, to stifle a wish that had flashed into my imagination. His death!

Silwan was very attached to me, whether or not he thought I was his savior from the nightmares that pursued him. But what about my nightmares? Who could save me from them? What about the strange creatures that besieged us as they besieged

Saint Anthony? The religious narrative was merciful to the saint and saved him. Tales always require heroes. But Max Ernst doesn't tell us the ending that he chose for his saint, besieged by fatal jaws in the painting before departing. Silwan was no hero. Defeated peoples have no heroes.

Sometimes I thought that all Silwan's talk about his supernatural ability to speak with animals could be true. He was friends with Guevara, and spoke to him all the time, and Guevara sat facing him for long periods, growling softly every now and then, or barking softly. Perhaps both of them were escaping frightening creatures in a never-ending diabolical game. I stopped writing. I needed to sit there idly and indefinitely as I waited for something unknown. I needed time to pass slowly so that I could shed my confusion. I needed to carefully inspect my feelings, to wash them with the purity that was diminishing around me, to rinse them of the dirt that had soiled them and to hang them up on a clothesline over which a burning Baghdadi sun would shine to purify them from the frightening hallucinations that had clung to them.

The days fell like leaves without a sound in this city. They died quickly, leaving only ashes behind. Daily life was fragile, surrounded by lies and fear. I was cloistered among ghosts that came from a very long past that had been erased, chapters written by our ancestors, leaving us to complete what they had begun, to record our lives with the merit they deserved.

I felt no desire to leave the large sitting room. I felt secure among the ghosts of the past, although I was sure that Mamluka was standing behind the door, even after Silwan had gone in search of Guevara.

She seemed unable to be patient any longer. I sensed her movement. When she wanted something she became restless and moved in a way I knew well. Her anxiety this time was intense and edgy, and she didn't wait for my response. After two quick knocks at the door, she stormed in and stood before me with poisoned questions in her eyes. The room was almost dark, now that the day had passed, as Cavafy promised in his exhausting journey in search of Ithaca. Noting my dogged silence, she said, "I must go. Do you want me to bring you anything?"

I remained silent. She seemed hesitant, tense, anxious. She said with some embarrassment, "Tomorrow at eleven o'clock some guests who want to speak to you about something that they said is of interest to you will come. They came about an hour ago, but I didn't want to disturb your private chat with Silwan. Your chat went on for a long time, so they decided to leave and told me they'd come again tomorrow at eleven in the morning."

She kept the door ajar as she left, instead of shutting it, as though she was saying, "Enough of that, leave this room of the dead." That's what Mamluka had been calling that room since my mother's death. But I remained sitting there, I don't know for how long. The city's nonchalance about time and its importance was taking hold of me, and I was afflicted with the same emptiness that permeated it.

CHAPTER 2

DISAPPEARANCE

ARNOLD BÖCKLIN: *ISLAND OF THE DEAD*

After having dinner with Silwan, I slept unexpectedly well. I petted Guevara a little to assuage my guilt for ignoring him for a long time and went to bed with a sense of psychological and physical lightness. I didn't think about the mysterious visitors that Mamluka had told me about until I noticed her moving around the mansion with a restlessness that I wanted to attribute to her anxiety and fear of the letter that only consisted of a bullet and a number. But it looked to me like there was something she knew and didn't want to tell me about. She was never in the habit of scolding Guevara and shooing him away, because she was the one to feed and pet him before gently pushing him into the garden and jokingly asking him to pursue and keep away the evil spirits trying to get close to us.

She didn't speak to me, although she made an effort to stay near me. Was she expecting me to confess my anxiety, fear, or other feelings to her? She didn't even sit in her usual way close to Silwan, of whom she was very fond. She was in the habit of squatting, leaning her back against the wall of the large, neglected veranda, dragging on a cigarette in her almost toothless mouth as though she wanted to swallow the fire inside it. From afar, she seemed as though she was listening to Silwan's ravings, but she wasn't really doing that. She simply considered what she was doing as part of her duty toward him since his return without his sanity from "there."

I sometimes felt guilty that I didn't know anything about that creature who had helped bring us up, except that her rank had been higher than the other servants who had worked for us. But who was she, really? That was a secret I had never found out. For sure, my mother, who had been dead a long time, had known a lot more about her than I did. Was she happy living among us, quickly responding to our requests without hesitation? I had no idea, but I did know that she'd been an indispensable part of our lives.

But as she served us breakfast that day, things were different. I asked about the jam, so she fetched it and put it in front of me rather irritably. Her irritability prompted me to refrain from asking about why the bread was cold, or why the eggs were cooked in a way I didn't like, or about the brown sugar I liked to have with my morning tea. These things didn't used to happen. Even her body odor was strange that day. Mamluka's body odor was distinctive. It reminded me of cactus fruit.

Her sphinx-like features hadn't changed since I'd learned to recognize faces, voices, and objects, except for the changes that time causes, but we don't notice them in those we see every day. She hadn't had any children, and I didn't ever remember seeing her talking intimately to Jawad, her husband. It sometimes seemed to me as though she deliberately humiliated him by ordering him to prune the plants in the garden or make sure that the fruit trees were pollinated. She would issue her orders curtly, then walk away as though she were talking to a stranger. He would carry out her orders without a word or an objection. She didn't eat with him, taking his food out to him in the garden, sitting next to him as he ate, and smoking voraciously without talking to him. I never saw her smile at him or direct a flirtatious look or gesture at him. It was a strange relationship for a couple that had been married for a long time. She had once worn vividly colored clothes, but then started wearing navy blue, then black. Her face had taken on a puckered frown that was most visible at the corners of her mouth.

My grandfather once threw a huge party in the garden to which he invited many guests of different nationalities. A stage was set up for the band, which played on until the early hours of the next day. The guests danced, drank, and ate the food that was on offer on the long tables that had been set up along the edges of the brilliantly lit garden.

That party took place two years after the young king had been dragged through the streets of the city, which had begun to experience the rise of barbarity and the familiarization of murder. My grandfather had intended such a big party to restore normality He had wanted to cleanse the remains of the blood that had polluted all the inhabitants of the city, whether as perpetrators, supporters, spectators, or the frightened. He threw that party even though the streets of the city still echoed with the loud shouts of the legions of demagogues who had filled the air with slogans of death, hatred, and intellectual shabbiness.

Mamluka had been the actual supervisor and organizer of that party. She was everywhere, fulfilling all the requests of the many guests, moving around energetically like a bee. Everyone acknowledged how expertly she had managed that special event. After the party, my mother had gifted Mamluka with a gold ring that she had worn on the little finger of her left hand. She still wore it.

I remembered how she had taken each of us children by the hand and led us to our bedrooms. I was naughtier and more stubborn than my siblings, so I refused to go with her and insisted that I wanted to attend the party till the end. That wasn't an option, of course. She wasn't hard on me. She just gently carried me, put me in bed, and said warmly, "It's no use being stubborn, darling. You must sleep now. When you grow up, you'll be the belle of the ball." She shut the door and went away. But the echo of her sentence, full of promise, stuck in my mind. I couldn't sleep that night. After the lights went out in the mansion's bedroom quarters, I jumped out of bed and headed for the window overlooking the garden. My room was on the second floor. I pushed the curtain aside and was bathed in the light coming from below. The men and women were wearing beautiful clothes, and jewelry glittered around the ladies' necks and wrists. There were groups of them here and there, carrying drinks. The dance floor was full of men and women who swayed and danced to lovely music, which I could still hear as I remembered the occasion. After that night, I wanted to grow up with magical speed so I could have the honor of staying up at my grandfather's glamorous party, full of that attractive outpouring of light that intensified the darkness surrounding the mansion and gave the palm groves ringing it a strange look. The tops of the trees seemed to me like frightening ghosts coming from beyond the palm grove. I looked away from them and refocused my gaze on the party. My dazzling grandfather was talking to a group of men, in the midst of whom stood a slim foreign woman, whom I saw heading for the dance floor with my father.

As the years passed, I grew sorrowfully certain that I wouldn't be the belle of the ball, as Mamluka had promised, and that someone would stand between me and the title that she had given me that night.

Most of the palm groves that the ghosts had emerged from were subsequently cut down and replaced by ugly buildings that were devoid of any taste. They kept increasing in number with an ugly chaos that turned those previous days into irretrievable memories.

It had been the last party of its kind. My grandfather died a year later, followed by my grandmother with unexpected speed. Since that night, I had continued to imagine the guests filling the real darkness with a virtual brilliance. Ever since then, I had stopped being one person and became two: Ghosnelban, who longed to be at a ball like the one she watched in her childhood, and another who recalled the fear of the surrounding darkness as a black prophecy that continued to scare me. I had discovered the danger of the darkness that was expanding around us and closing in slowly and fatally. Tiamat, the goddess of blindness and chaos in the Babylonian myth of creation, came to mind.

To me, that night had been the last of our Scheherazade

nights. It was followed by my first bitter experience: loss. I had to adapt to it and get used to its recurring taste, which grew more bitter with every loss.

I gathered up the papers I had written on the previous day. Before going into the large sitting room to continue writing, I told Mamluka not to let anyone interrupt me. I definitely didn't intend this to apply to Silwan and Guevara. Mamluka gave me a stupid look laced with slight disapproval. Then she impatiently uttered two words: "the guests." It was all she said that morning. Although I remembered what she was referring to, I didn't pay much attention to it, I don't know why.

I went into the sitting room, closed the door behind me, and started looking over my papers. After slightly more than an hour, I decided to take a break. I sat before Swiss artist Arnold Böcklin's painting *Island of the Dead.* As I sat in pleasurable contemplation, Mamluka burst in on me like a storm. She was tense, as though she had some very weighty news, and said to me in a voice that seemed to be shaking with emotion, "They've arrived."

Her behavior surprised me, but I ignored it, although it bothered me, because I was the captain of that sinking ship, and everyone's future on it depended on me.

The mansion had until then been ruled by strict rules of etiquette that had accumulated over time, becoming more like laws that could not be infringed. Ever since we had become conscious of our lives, things had been done that way. None of us had ever questioned those rules, or considered changing them, even if some of us had been bothered by such strictness. None of us even objected to them, and that included Silwan and me. Anyone who hadn't liked those rules would have to leave the mansion, which was actually what happened, but I decided to return to that story later.

One of those rules was that guests were ushered into the rooms that were commensurate with their importance, social status, and the nature of their relationship with the mansion's inhabitants. Mamluka knew this well because it was part of her job, and it was unthinkable that she would make a mistake about it. Friends and acquaintances were received in the small reception room, the large veranda, or the garden if the weather was suitable. My mother's friends would visit her in the large kitchen overlooking the back garden, in which Jawad planted all kinds of vegetables that were consumed in the mansion and tended all the exotic, sweet-smelling flowers that my mother and grandmother had brought from all over the world. The women chitchatted about the secrets of homes and families in that large kitchen, overlooking that beautiful view, away from the eyes of men and children. Our personal friends were shown to our personal rooms. As for the large reception room, it was only frequented by official guests or very important ones and was the venue of the long-gone gatherings my grandfather hosted on the first Thursday of every month until his death.

My father and my grandfather before him had played a major political role in the country, so my father liked to take his guests into the library, where the shelf walls held hundreds of Arabic and English books and the air still seemed to hold the aroma of tobacco and the remnants of political chats. My grandfather's main concern had been to avoid getting carried away by extremist political trends, both on the Left and on the

Right. But that independent dream ended, and the country had fallen into a morass of conflicts that ended up with the ugliest form of dictatorship, followed by chaos and ruination.

As I got up to meet the guests in the smaller sitting room, I was surprised to see that Mamluka has left the door open, allowing two women and a man into the room.

Such rude and strange behavior made me uncomfortable. It was a painful and inexcusable violation of the mansion's traditions, which predated my birth, particularly since Mamluka knew those traditions well. Actually, she was the one who regulated the way in which guests were received at the mansion in a disciplined way, unless she was told in advance that an exception was to be made. Were they hiding behind her as she told me they'd arrived? How could they behave that way, barging in on me with no regard for my privacy?

Their behavior gave rise to a rejection of them even before I had taken a proper look at them.

I stood in astonishment trying to catch Mamluka's eye, but her shifting gaze avoided mine as she tried to sidestep my anger at her behavior. Who were those people she'd just let in to the large reception room?

That room had hosted personalities such as former prime ministers Nouri al-Said and Jaafar al-'Askari; literary figures like al-Rasafi and al-Zahawi; artists like Afifa Iskandar and Salima Murad Basha; foreign diplomats, and many other such figures. Its history was being insulted. But I needed to understand why Mamluka was acting so strangely, so I held in my anger and forced myself to smile sternly in a manner that looked like I might explode at any moment.

The three of them stood before me, unable to restrain their curiosity. Their glances slithered around the room like snakes in a disgusting way. I felt violated and helpless. Mamluka shut the door, and I had no choice anymore. I gestured them toward a corner in the room, seething with rage.

The two women were wrapped in black from head to toe. They daintily whipped off their abayas in a practiced way, and the place was filled with a concentrated scent of rose, which I used to smell when accompanying my mother to visit graves that had become holy shrines. Frankly, I was scared during those visits because of all the crowding and the strange faces of the women in black. My mother would beg us to accompany her on those visits, and everyone tried to avoid them.

Out of sympathy, I would agree in the end. My mother was very keen on keeping the vows she made. Only those visits to the imams and holy men could rescue her from the fear and black thoughts that would assail her after a nightmare or when a black crow squawked three times in the garden on its way to the adjacent Armenian cemetery. I was always frightened by the sight of the weeping women hanging onto the golden windows of the imams' shrines. The shrines meant nothing to me as I stood before them. They seemed like an ornate gate of secrets, with women trying to bury their fears in their golden-colored cages. Perhaps if the religious figures to whom the shrines had been built could speak, they would have disapproved of such customs, which were based on myths confused with facts, believed by those that were unable to confront their problems. So they turned instead to myth-making practices that would transform their fears into a certitude similar to a giant spider web that enfolded many generations in its sticky fabric. We had stuck to it, surrendering to our terrifying fate, becoming incapable of any initiative

Could all those women have shared the same fears and obsessions that plagued my mother? As an adult, I've come to know that superstition is an accumulation of people's experiences, mingled with collective hallucination and mystery that require divine intervention to stop the hell of the approaching evil!

My father repeatedly said that my mother had not always been like that, because she was an educated lady. But following the barbaric killing of the young king and the concomitant atrocities she had experienced and actually seen, she had changed, turning into a superstitious woman, even hallucinating and believing she could see approaching evil in a way we could not!

At those holy shrines, my mother would nervously and reverentially draw close to the golden windows with crowds of frightened women. She would ask me to remain close by so that I would not get lost amid the crowds that resembled an ever-flowing river. She would cover her nose with a silk handkerchief to keep out the odor of jostling bodies, and she would timidly insert herself among the other women. She would only become composed after touching the imam's grave and hurriedly reciting some verses from the Qur'an, keeping her eye on me all the time. To me, religion merely signified large question marks and a definite desire to avoid all the human masses that practiced it with a kind of delusional acceptance. Although I was influenced by my mother's piety, I thought it should differ from the spectacle of such myth-laden rituals.

The scent of concentrated rose, black, loud sobbing, outstretched arms, my mother's lips as she muttered prayers, and even the tense whispered fears and wishes that could be heard—I recalled all of it with the scent of the two women, which savagely spread through the sitting room, once graced with a visit by Abdul Ilah, the regent to the throne of the murdered king, whose body had been dismembered with almost incomparable brutality!

I began to watch them, but I was, in fact, watching myself even more. I had an obsession that I could not control with making my behavior perfect for purposes of comparison that would give me the space to be distinctively superior to others. I had learned in my childhood not to allow a random or uncalculated look or a misplaced glance to affect the intensity of the smile on my face. I sat before them with my back very straight and my neck held high to emphasize the difference between myself and them. I placed my right hand over my left hand to hide a diamond ring on my finger. My hair was gathered back, my legs were together, and my expression was a mixture of inquisitive disgust and superiority, which I did not try to conceal.

I had never regarded others as inferior, but a barrier sprang up between us because of the way they had come in to see me, and their glances, which betrayed a kind of envy over the contents of the sitting room.

The older woman bore a strong resemblance to Mamluka, and I wondered if she was her sister or a relative. She had the same pursed lips as Mamluka—an unmistakable sign that they were related. They also had similar noses. The woman seemed older than Mamluka, and her glances betrayed a determination that bordered on cruelty. She was wrapped in black like a shield against life. Her head was covered by a shiny black scarf, and where it was tied at the left corner of her head there was a golden brooch with a light blue fragment at the tip. The words she had rehearsed well in advance were gathered at the corner of her mouth as she waited for a suitable opportunity to proceed. There was a look of firm determination in her eyes.

As for the younger woman, it was difficult to determine her real age because of the fat that had accumulated in many corners of her nearly square body. In all cases, she was younger than me. The golden threads in her headscarf mitigated its black hostility. The scarf surrounded her round face but didn't completely cover her hair, in what may have been a deliberate gesture of coquetry. The scarf pressed into her face, causing her cheeks, which were painted very red, to stand out, and which, together with red lipstick that seemed to have been hastily applied, made her look like a clown.

Her gaze flitted in all directions, then rested on me as she examined me with a brazenness that bordered on insolence. She pressed her palms together as though trying to control her nervousness and confusion. She wore many golden rings of different sizes on all her fingers. She proudly glanced at her reddish gold bracelets every now and then, whenever they collided and made a ringing sound. Something in her face made her seem friendlier than the woman who resembled Mamluka. Perhaps it was her youth. She did not hide her joy as she looked at the ornaments in the sitting room. She had obviously seen nothing like them before.

The younger woman edged closer to the man until her shoulder touched his and she nudged him whenever she wanted to draw his attention to the things she thought were beautiful, but he paid her no attention.

The man looked to be in his late forties. He had put too much grease on his thick hair in a cheap way that was inappropriate for age. Specks of dust from the street had stuck to his hair like dandruff.

His features bore the same cruelty as the older woman's, and he had the same pursed lips, with a thin moustache above them. His glances were full of desire, prurience, and greed. He wore a Chinese-made khaki suit of the kind that was abundantly available, a white shirt, and a brightly colored necktie. His shoes were a yellowish brown that had faded because of the dust, and he wore white sports socks. He looked like an advertisement for cheap Chinese goods. Men who wore rings put me off, and he was wearing two very large silver rings on the third and smallest fingers of his right hand.

The women were shifting their gazes between me and the living room and its ornaments. But he focused on me with a prurience that he could not control, and I felt as though he were undressing me and biting my body the way animals bit bodies in Silwan's tales.

I remained silent awaiting the scenario they had arrived with before Mamluka had ushered them in, despite the sudden anxiety that made my stomach contract, and my fear for the "last bastion of civilization," as my mother called our mansion.

I gave them an inquiring look in the hope that it would encourage them to bring up the reason for their visit. The older woman glanced right and left, as though she were giving the start signal. No one else saw it besides me, but they felt it. The man straightened himself slightly and glanced away from the sensitive parts of my body, focusing on my face. The fat woman's movements ceased, and her friendly smile disappeared.

The woman who resembled Mamluka began to speak in a voice that sounded like a hoarse man's, possibly because she was a heavy smoker. She said the three of them were inhabitants of Baghdad and elaborated on their origins and lineage.

I could not accept the idea that they we were inhabitants of the same city. My Baghdad was different from their Baghdad. The name sounded different, depending on who was uttering it. Every person has a concept of the city that he or she dwells in and a concept of a what a city is. She seemed to have used that introduction to give me the impression that we were from the same city, our dispositions were alike, and therefore, we had a great deal in common!

Then she said that she knew me through her sister, Mamluka.

This did not surprise me, given the strong resemblance between them and the recent strangeness in Mamluka's behavior. Nevertheless, I blushed and looked away in spite of myself. The woman noticed my moment of weakness and stretched her body a whole inch higher as she began to talk about her son, Fadhil, gazing at him proudly. She mentioned his "record of struggle" against the dictatorial regime, which had been uprooted by the army of occupation. She kept emphatically bringing up the crimes of the defunct era to create common ground between us, using the logic that suffering at the hands of all the country's illegitimate regimes was something we all shared, and her son had "struggled" to topple dictatorship—hence, we were "all" the victims of the same regime. She attributed everything that had happened to her son's "struggle" and that of his comrades, prompting me to take a good look at him to see if I could detect the image of the "struggler" in him. But all I could see was an insignificant, impatient man who wanted to possess my body, and with it, our mansion. I almost smiled with merriment as I searched for an adjective that would suit him. Everything about him was fake. The only thing his clothes had in common were their poor choice: the over-sized accessories, his stupid occasional glance at his gold watch and the vulgar way in which he was sitting, with open legs as though he were preparing to urinate, or perhaps so that I could see his great sex instrument. I smiled inwardly at this suitor, who had not once thought of smiling at a strange lady sitting opposite him.

What was that stupid lady talking about?

I glanced away for them for a moment, and my thoughts were immersed in that strange group of people that claimed to have rid us of dictatorship to put the country that I loved on the road to modern democracy.

During her boring talk about her son, Mamluka's sister neglected to introduce the other woman who was sitting next to her, and I had to patiently listen to her account of her son's mythical heroism, while he showed no interest in what she was saying, moving his gaze between my bosom and his large golden watch. It seemed he was used to his mother's boring chatter.

I too could not suppress my boredom and impatience with her propaganda festival. I knew full well that there were no heroes this country, which had been led from one defeat to another by its rulers, let alone that unremarkable man whose mother was talking about him with such enthusiasm. I no longer hid my displeasure with the real reason for their visit. It did not seem as though they had come to seek financial help, and they must have known that our properties had been nationalized and confiscated a long time ago, and that everything we had managed to keep had been confiscated to support the last war effort, which had sent hundreds of thousands of young men to mass graves, leaving those who had survived mutilated.

The woman's gibberish finally came to end and she fell silent. A comfortable and restful calm ensued. I remained silent in the hope that they would get bored or would understand the meaning of my silence and return to where they had come from. But Mamluka entered the room carrying glasses of cold orange juice on a beautiful copper tray that I had brought with me from the Moroccan city of Meknas. I was grateful for the gesture, although she had not acted on any instructions I had given her. As I had expected, she did not look at me.

Everyone sipped their refreshing drink. Then the older woman made her move. She set down her glass slowly and quietly on the table between us, and in a voice that she tried to make as tender and clear as possible, said, "We've come here today in the hope that you will not turn us down, my child."

She looked at me, and before I could open my mouth, she quickly stabbed me again. "We would like to ask for your hand in marriage for my son Fadhil."

Her manner of speaking and her tone made it clear that this was no ordinary request that could be simply decided with a yes or no answer. Its effect was more like that of the rodent bites described by Silwan, or those that ate away at the Marib Dam, destroying the civilization around it forever.

I almost shouted back, "You mean the struggler!" But the implications of her request dulled my mind, paralyzed my tongue, and drained the blood from my face. My lips froze. I wanted to pick up the glass of orange juice and wet my parched lips, but I would have preferred to die of thirst than to go along with their ceremony of insults.

I felt no hatred toward them. Perhaps I did not want to give them my hatred, because that would have meant building an entity that brought me together with them, and that was the last thing I wanted. They were "others," and recognition of that was all I could give them. That was the only way I could deal with them.

Meanwhile, their eyes were keenly on me. The fake man was examining my body again with an avidness I did not know how to stop. The fat lady broke out into a cheap, flirtatious smile. The older woman's features became harsher and crueler, as if to threaten me if I refused.

My thirst for something much more than the drink beside me forced me to remain silent, although I wanted to say something that would end the farce. The air of anticipation allowed me to hear their quickening breaths. Silence exposed their inability to confiscate me in the same way that our lives had been confiscated, but it also overwhelmed me with humiliation and defeat. Here, in the large reception room in which everything was part of my history, as my ancestors and forebears were surely watching me, I was being insulted in a way that had been impossible for me to imagine!

After losing hope that I would respond, Mamluka's sister spoke again.

"My only son has been appointed as an ambassador to Greece, and he will need an educated woman like you to stand by his side and support him when he is away from home."

For the first time, she gestured to the woman sitting beside her and added, "As for Intissar, she will remain with me, because I am old and unable to take care of their children on my own."

This time, the words "their children" jumped into my head and hardened onto my frozen lips, and I felt I had lost the ability to speak. Intissar seized the opportunity. She was clearly unable to remain silent any longer, and stuttered some words I could barely understand,

"Yes, we have four beautiful children, God bless them, and I have no objections to his marrying you."

She spoke as though everything had been settled, and all that was left was to decide the date of the wedding. She threw her mother-in-law a quick glance to measure her reaction. Her words had gone down well, and her mother-in-law smiled at her, slightly diminishing the harshness of her face. The future bridegroom was emboldened and waded into the festival of humiliation, composing his sentences with grand-sounding words he deemed worthy of the occasion.

"Only a high-class lady can stand by my side when I'm there. A lady who knows how to behave. We want to convey an honorable image of the new democratic Iraq. I understand from my aunt Mamluka that you have a good command of several foreign languages, and that is exactly what is required."

He laughed briefly, then continued, "I never had the opportunity to study at university, because I had vowed early on to dedicate my life to saving the country from dictatorship."

"But it was the Americans who overthrew the regime?" I said, hardly knowing how I had said this to him, to them.

But he continued his pre-packaged talk, as though he had not heard me.

When he had finished his presentation, he leaned back and moved his legs further apart, looking toward me insolently, as though to say, "Go on, say yes—you won't find anyone better than me to accept you and grant you his protection in this city, which has embraced our democracy."

I was so angry that I did not feel their real presence before me as I tried to examine the superficial mud out of which that disgusting creature had been molded, prompting him to believe that he was necessary in life. Truly, did the lives of such human beings have meaning?

My god, how unbearable the whole situation was. I rose from my place as though stung and stood by the door, signaling them to leave with an ugly and crushing expression of anger on my face. For a short while, they were in disbelief and hesitant, failing to comprehend how a "fool" like me could miss out on such a golden opportunity. The older woman gathered up her abaya slowly as she struggled to present herself as someone enjoying a higher status than me. Her pathetic attempts failed because she did not understand that putting a bullet in a miserable envelope and owning a bag of ill-gotten money were not enough to earn a status that others would appreciate and recognize.

After I ascertained that they were departing, I automatically headed for a beautiful antique cupboard that my grandfather had brought from Afghanistan. We kept our alcoholic drinks in it, and I mixed myself a strong martini and gulped it down all at once in the hope that it would dull the anger that was almost strangling me. I was not used to drinking alcohol, particularly at that time of day, but that was no longer important. To hell with all the rules. Not in my worst nightmares had it occurred to me that the city's worn-out garbage would float in and force its way into my life in such an awful way!

Following their departure, my feelings of contempt and revulsion prompted me to search for Mamluka. Silwan stood before me with a look in his eyes that begged for some of my time. Guevara, who was behind him, sensed my anger and grew tense. I said to Silwan curtly, "Not now, please."

I searched for her everywhere she might be, but she was nowhere to be found.

I stood in the kitchen, which I only rarely entered following my mother's death. Mamluka had tidied up the kitchen in her usual neat, organized way, and a degree of calm came over me as I wondered what I should do about her. Should I fire her, or should I simply scold her for her insolent behavior toward me, toward us?

My father had always told us, "Remaining silent in difficult times is in itself a weapon against insolence and incomprehension." At that moment, I could not understand what was occurring. How had those people dared to be so insolent? Had our lives become so inconsequential? Should I reproach her, although she was incapable of understanding such matters?

In the past, only a limited category of people had behaved insolently and rudely toward others and tried to humiliate them, but they were reviled. But now that had become "normal" behavior for the majority of people, particularly those who had learned from their humiliators.

The alcohol worked and it gave me a refreshing feeling of lightness, prompting me to smile back at Silwan as he headed toward the garden with Guevara, where he would sit beneath the black fig tree to recite his hallucinations to the faithful dog, who would fall asleep, unconcerned with the animals that ate the bodies of the defeated soldiers near the country's borders.

I returned to the sitting room more determined to continue writing our story.

I once again sat and studied Böcklin's *Island of the Dead*. What could that painting tell me at such a difficult time? Death is disappearance, and the artist had linked them after a rich widow asked him to embody her grief following the death of her beloved husband. Grief, loss, anguish, sadness, a feeling of impotence, and all the other emotions are part of the symphony of pain that disturbs her sleep and renders her incapable of accepting her husband's death. His eternal disappearance has plunged her into grief, notwithstanding her ability to achieve anything she wants with her money, beauty, and social status. But none of them have been any use to her. Death is the only adversary that she has been unable to vanquish. Death has vanquished her because it has a unique weapon she can do nothing about: disappearance!

Böcklin has painted the widow cloaked in white, standing in a small boat in front of the body of her beloved as the boat heads toward the desolate Island of the Dead, which appears as though it had been a small happy city blighted by a divine destructive curse that changed it into a forsaken place, a symbol of disappearance that only leaves anguish in its wake. She travels there to surrender the body of her beloved and confess her final impotence and total submission to the power of death and its stunning ability to cause disappearance.

The inability to forget someone who has disappeared from your life means that it will keep gnawing at the wound, preventing it from healing.

The idea of disappearance threw my memory back to events that had occurred a long time before but had not been erased, digging into the indelible wound: my older sister Julnar, who one day decided to join the Iraqi Communist Party and had picked a communist man as a partner!

A destructive earthquake had hit deep within our family history and shaken the ground beneath our feet, which we had thought were firmly well protected. As time went by, the wound became a strict, ironclad taboo that no one could approach or touch. Nevertheless, none of us could forget the effects of the tragedy, even though we pretended it did not exist. Julnar's irrevocable departure deprived us of complete rest— a lead-colored privation with which one cannot acclimatize or become familiar, something offputtingly protuberant.

Julnar refused to leave us. She remained sitting in our agitated minds and contradictory feelings that were full of questions. We tried to regain her and distance her in equal measure. We forgave her and condemned her. Her desolately empty place forced us not to forget.

The men in the family and their close friends used to sit in the large sitting room and talk about the disappearance of the city in which we had all been born and grown up, and of the disappearance of many people we remembered, whom we had lost, who had immigrated. But they never talked about Julnar's disappearance. The women silently exchanged confused looks. Her image was strongly present in everyone's consciousness, whether those who spoke of the city's disappearance or those who looked down so that no one could see their tears. Julnar and the act of disappearance had become one!

After her disappearance from our lives, the process of turning her into a hazy memory became our preoccupation. We all actively participated in that cruel exercise with a rare ingenuity. We wanted to delete the shame of her action, not by regret but by forgetfulness and uprooting. Her photographs disappeared from our photograph collection, her clothes, her jewelry, her bed, her mirror, her books, the vinyl records she listened to, and the raisins she liked could never again be found in our kitchen.

None of those actions caused any shock. It all happened silently within our sight and hearing and with our connivance until it became necessary to ask, had she, whose name we could no longer mention, lived among us, or had she merely been a dream or a lie?

The only thing that gave the lie to such deceit was a wardrobe in a deserted room to which my mother kept the keys. We called it "the black memory box." My mother did not want to forget the tragedy, and she turned it into a barrier between herself and true happiness, as though she wanted to temper her freedom, joy, laughter, and the colors of her clothes. She would open the cupboard every now and then to breathe in the scent of loss and damage and redefine the borders of grief and pain that had grown fainter in her memory. She never allowed herself to get over it, or to forget her failure to bring up her daughter to respect inherited traditions that were completely intolerant of self-indulgence. She held herself solely responsible for the loss. Someone had to volunteer for such a difficult task, and she did!

The whole thing amounted to the manufacture of a lie that we were required to be the first to believe. It started the day my mother, with the help of Mamluka, wrapped some sweets in silk handkerchiefs to distribute to neighbors and acquaintances, in accordance with prevalent traditions, signaling that Julnar had married with the family's consent. From the witch's kitchen arose the steam of a lie that covered our lives with a foggy lack of clarity and a fear of confronting the truth. We all hastened to cook it and stir the magic pot from which the steam arose, obsessed with the fear that the steam would condense into water droplets that would fall on us.

My father was no less pained by the tragedy. After Julnar's resounding disappearance, his smile became a rarity in our lives. When we had guests, his beautiful smile would appear, and we would peak at it as though it were sunlight we had been deprived of for a sin we had not committed.

My father and mother outdid themselves in taking responsibility, although they certainly did not discuss Julnar at all. Their feelings of guilt mingled with the bitterness of loss turned into a kind of masochistic pleasure that captivated them as time went by.

Julnar had not been an ordinary member of our family. She was the most brilliant, most intelligent, most refined, and most mysterious of us.

My grandfather had loved her very much. She had been his favorite, and he had hoped that she would carry the family's heavy glory. He took her with him everywhere and enjoyed her company. The same was true of my father and even of me, although I could not hide the fact that I was jealous of her and loved her in equal measure. Her departure left a white indefinable void in my life. I used to sit next to her in the garden as she painted her nails with a light red polish. She would have a glass of hot milk beside her and a tape recorder out of which floated the voice of Fairuz, which she made me adore. She would glance up every now and then to give me a bright smile that made me happy. Strangely, I never knew why.

Disappearance causes so much pain. It gives one a feeling of impotence, the inability to take the right decisions, sadness, burning regret, and all that is harmful!

At first, I may have been the only one who tried to resist the cruel act of making her disappear. I knew that such a decision was irrevocable, and that it had imposed itself on all of us. Once I ascertained that the days and evenings would pass in her absence, I decided to fortify myself against forgetfulness. I knew that I couldn't separate myself from the rest of the family by eschewing complicity in her forced disappearance, so I decided to secretly keep some of her books. I wanted to hold on to my sister, but without her action or the person she had decided to marry, whose name I could not even recall!

I secretly hid the books that I had saved from the fire of forced erasure in my room to help me preserve the memory of the sister whom I had loved and envied. At night, when I was sure that everyone else was asleep, I would bring them out and touch and smell their covers, hoping they would help me to solve the puzzle of her disappearance. I studied certain passages that she had underlined in pencil and tried to comprehend them so that I could trace her thoughts, as though the secret of her disappearance were hiding among those sentences and lines, which seemed unintelligible and complex to me at the time. Marx, Engels, Lenin, Hegel, Søren Kierkegaard, Sartre, Saadi Youssef, Hannah Arendt, Ghassan Kanafani, and others. But those lines remained beyond my understanding, frugal and meager, complicating my understanding of the puzzle that had occurred. So I started out rejecting those writers and ended up hating them. They had stolen my sister from me.

I would go back to those books and lines every now and then, not to understand them, which I did when I grew up, but to call up the feelings of pain, the tears my mother was careful to conceal from us, the lines of pain that her absence had etched on my father's forehead, our collective debacle, the feel of the fifteen-pound notes that Julnar had forgotten forever between the pages of *Being and Nothingness*, the scent of her favorite perfume—Chanel, the nicotine of her cigarettes, drops of the coffee she used to drink, the ink of her pens, remnants of her mysterious thoughts, her decision to run away, the effects of burying her beneath the earth of forgetfulness, the renewed feeling of a wound that would not heal.

I didn't know where she was. None of us did, or more accurately, none of us wanted to. My father did not isolate her memory behind an iron curtain, but he obscured it with a wall of thick fog that we were terrified of penetrating or approaching. Since the day that the sweets had been fraudulently distributed, Julnar's name was no longer mentioned. She suddenly turned into an absent pronoun: "she." When it was necessary to refer to her, it would be done in whispered tones, as though we were committing a sin!

The rumors were ceaseless. We heard that after the collapse of the national front that the communists had set up with their Baathist persecutors, and the season of hunting them down with all the other leftists began, she fled to one of the countries that were still socialist at that time. Then we heard that she had been seen fighting in the rugged northern mountains as part of the "Ansar" movement after her husband was killed in the Dhofar Mountains of Oman. The last person who claimed to have seen her said that she was working as a teacher of Arabic in Algeria.

Were we really interested in getting news of her, or were we searching for news of her defeats to prove to ourselves that we were right and that such a black fate awaited anyone who dared to leave the haven of the mansion and history? I don't know.

In the end, Julnar turned into a confused dream, and that was it.

Sometimes I wondered why she hadn't tried to contact us all those years, but I quickly retreated from that thorny question—because had I been in her place, I would not have tried. How would I justify the big deception I had been part of with false slogans and turn the feeling of disappointment into words?

My father's sad frown remained with him until his death, and he was unwilling to forgive. We knew this, and so did she. He might have forgiven anything else, but not embracing communist thinking. He had sensed the opportunism and cruelty of their leaders from the beginning. Had he lived to experience the shameful day of occupation, he would have seen them jumping onto the occupation's tanks to get into weak government positions, and he would have felt happy that they had finally been so blatantly exposed and declared final victory over them. If by some twisted turn of fate I were to meet Julnar, my only question to her would be "Was the price that you paid, and that you forced us all to pay with for the sake of such people, worth it?"

It was impossible to understand how the beautiful, aristocratic Julnar, a graduate of Al-Hikma University College could turn into a fighter in the rugged mountains or into a teacher in an Algerian village, or...!

I read the literature of communist thought as I traced the tracks of the mirage that had swallowed up Julnar. I surveyed their arts as part of my studies at the Fine Arts Academy, but I never for a moment felt close to such thinking, which clung to certainty, inevitability, and violation of human nature, which eagerly revolts against all that is constant. I hated their crude arts, which were superficial to the point of banality.

It was Thursday, the day for the traditional ritual that our family had observed for three successive generations, and perhaps longer. It was the day on which all members of the family would come to the mansion. Sometimes I felt the burden of that day, but on other days I looked forward to it, depending on the general mood and the events we were passing through. But irrespective of the situation, we never missed a Thursday gathering. Even after Julnar's disappearance, my father did not break that rule unless we were traveling during the summer holidays, but even then the Thursday date would remain suspended in our mental calendars until our return.

That day, as we met and then dispersed, we were all seized by a feeling that it was the last Thursday. The collapse of that deeply rooted ritual gave us a feeling of failure and helplessness, particularly after bidding one another farewell. The shadow of the bullet hovered over us, causing us to wallow in the mud of defeat and to witness the disappearance of our existence and influence in this city, although we had contributed to the making of its golden glory.

Mamluka had perfectly made the arrangements necessary for that day and had then disappeared. I put the last remaining touches on those preparations in a manner befitting the last granddaughter remaining at the large mansion. Balqis and Rabab arrived early, which helped me. They had made a shopping date before coming, and before their husbands and children caught up with them, so I was able to talk to them before we were distracted by other things.

As soon as they came in, they sensed the prevailing atmosphere of tension, which I was unable to hide or dilute. Balqis asked about Mamluka, so I was forced to lie and say that she was sick. Rabab's mirthful laugh pleased me, and Rabab said,

"This is the first time I hear that Mamluka is sick." Balqis replied with some regret, "It's old age, my dear. Even Mamluka is getting older, and I used to think she was an ageless woman. She brought us all up and watched us getting married and having children, all while she was still working for us."

The conversation carefully moved on to other unimportant topics without focusing on anything specific. Silwan decided to spend the longest possible time with Guevara in the garden, as though he wanted to give us the opportunity to talk about the recent developments.

Balqis took a sip of coffee, then looked straight into my eyes and said, "Come on, Ghosnelban, tell us what it is that you're keeping to yourself—you're not good at hiding your anxiety."

"Why d'you think I'm hiding something?"

"Because I know you as well as I know myself. Something has happened, and you're trying to hide it."

I was suddenly seized by a wave of weakness that I couldn't control, and it almost made me cry. But I managed to stop it from breaking loose without my permission, which would have embarrassed me. My mother always said it was uncivilized to cry easily or to show real feelings. My confusion, or the signs of weakness that I had shown, took them by surprise. Rabab nervously lit a cigarette and said impatiently, "Do you want us to share your anxiety and apprehension without understanding its causes?"

I got up, visibly irritated, and walked toward the place I had hidden the threatening letter. I brought it and put it before them, between the two still-hot cups of coffee. Balqis turned it over cautiously. It took her some time to understand the implications of the bullet on the table. Her face drained of color, and one of them said, "Is that a murder threat?"

"Yes."

The silence that ensued was necessary to comprehend what had happened, and it was doubtful that words could explain and tidy up the chaos that had flooded our minds. It was the first time we had received a direct threat. In spite of the barbarism of all the political phases that had followed the murder of the young king, things had never reached such an uncontrollable low. It was necessary for me to regain the initiative because I had already known about it a day earlier. I cleared my throat to ensure that my voice would not let me down, then said, "And now?"

The question hovered over the room. I had not meant to ask it in that way, because I knew the situation was too grave to allow direct questions to be asked at a time when we had lost any influence over our lives and fates, which were controlled by strange dark hands, the like of which we had never experienced.

I suggested to Rabab that we postpone the matter until the men's arrival, so that we could consult them. I knew that she simply wanted to postpone the issue.

It took hours, and I exerted a lot of pressure to control my nerves. I was aware of how clever we were at pulling down heavy curtains over the things that bothered us. I also knew that I was the main, even the only, person responsible for taking the final decision. In fact, that became the case when the men found out about the issue. I was deluged with suggestions that could not be implemented. After much discussion, my conviction grew that neither my sisters, nor their husbands could come up with any solutions, not because they were less capable or daring or courageous than I was, but because coming up with solutions under such circumstances was very difficult, if not impossible.

I would have to deal with the problem on my own. Rabab's husband was an employee at the foreign ministry and was preparing to travel to Portugal with his family to take up the post of consul there. They hinted that under no circumstances would they return to the country. In other words, this would be a final migration. As for Balqis's husband, he was a pharmacist who had joined the Baath Party to secure his interests and told me that he was under surveillance, was periodically summoned for routine questioning by the committees tasked with rooting out the Baath Party, and that they too were thinking of moving away. I had not known that before.

So, I would have to face the approaching storm alone. I understood my relatives' circumstances, so I decided not to reveal to them the identity of the unwelcome visitors who had descended on me that morning courtesy of Mamluka. That piece of news would have intensified their feelings of humiliation, so I decided to spare them.

After that, I don't know why I felt that that I was the strongest among them, and it made me happy that they were depending on me fully to find a solution that was beyond my power. I had always been determined when it came to taking the decisions that I felt were correct, although I had never infringed on the traditional family taboos. That is why I remained acceptable, unlike Julnar, who had violated and broken all taboos.

Our talk during the rest of the evening was a valediction for Baghdad, which was disappearing before our eyes. We competed to paint the picture of utter destruction and our painful demise, a city that was disappearing, just like Julnar, who left nothing but whispers, mutterings, and rumors behind. But I also understood that the process of disappearance was not sudden, like a thunderbolt. It had occurred and taken shape before our eyes and consciousness. The symphony of painful disappearance began after the first military coup. As the coups continued and intensified, one phase would disappear, taking with it names, faces, families, traditions, patterns of behavior, monuments, elites, and statues, and a new more recent phase would emerge until we woke up one day to find that the city we knew no longer felt familiar and that we represented the remains of a city that practically no longer existed except in our memories—which were also disappearing, so that we began to doubt their existence, like the body being delivered by the mourner to the Island of the Dead in Böcklin's painting.

They had given me the freedom to act, although no one said so explicitly. But that was how we dealt with one another. Explicitness was the death of us, and I knew that whatever my decision would be, they would approve of it with gratitude.

I could not blame any of them. They were exactly like me, feeling naked, cold, and lost. I felt very sympathetic toward them. We were all in trouble. It was time to liquidate the heavy legacy, the family tradition, its entire history. We were all equally impotent.

At that moment of critical silence, Silwan came in, standing among us with his shy, broad smile, examining each of us in order to choose the right person to whom to narrate the deranged epic he was experiencing. He stood before us like a question that was open to all possibilities: What about him?

None of us dared look at the others. I saw them weeping as they ignored my mother's instructions to control our emotions. It occurred to me that she was watching us from heaven and crying with us about the horrifying fate that was testing our abilities to act in a time of recklessness in which all the concepts and established principles that we had known and had been brought up to respect were being turned on their head. It was a time that was larger than all of our knowledge, its paces controlled by the insane expansion of the militias that controlled the city and its weak, surrendering pulse, a time that was pushing us toward disappearance from the usurped city.

We were drowning in their violence like dead people that were being transported toward the Island of Fate by the woman in white. Disappearance was our fate, and we were helpless to resist it. Powers falling, and other opposing ones rising. Perhaps Julnar had been the smartest among us when she decided to disappear while she was sure we were still in our place. She could draw on her memory and take refuge in it during difficult times, as Silwan had done in the Desert of Death. But our disappearance would be as bitter as poison because we would not leave behind any traces that we could resort to and remember in the difficult days that lay ahead.

CHAPTER 3

LOVE

MAX LIEBERMANN: *SAMSON AND DELILAH*

Had I robbed him of his sacred halo?

That thought came into my head on the third day as I sat in the large sitting room and faced my grandfather's paintings, which I had come to see as a means of interpreting the puzzles in my life, rather than the puzzles of his life.

I knew that this was just babble on my part, but I liked the feeling of some meaningfulness, some power, even if it was an illusion. I needed it because there were those who wanted to throw me into a futile void.

As I opened my eyes that morning, the first thing I saw was my loneliness. Yes, accursed loneliness that over long years had with suspicious quietness managed to sneak into my pores, my thoughts, my decisions, and I had meekly succumbed to it and accurately organized my habits, which I had clung to as my mother had clung to the sacred golden windows. I had remained obsessed with keeping my behavior perfect down to the minutest detail, as though I were fulfilling a vow at a temple every day. I had consciously and unconsciously allowed myself to be thrust into the creeping loneliness that had seized control of me, like the snake that had slithered into Cleopatra's bed and killed her. It had all happened without any resistance from me, as I surrendered to a divinely ordained fate.

That morning, I saw my loneliness penetrating my soul like a sunbeam shining onto the floor of my room, like a heavenly message of light and pain, a message that would brook no denial. I was a lonely person without family, except for Silwan, who barely existed. No friends, no lover, no fatal diseases, no hope of anything, not even any hatred, no faith, and nothing to protect me from the terrifying feeling of loneliness. I was living in a city that had lost its memory and had been violated by hypocrites.

I was left with nothing but faint, deceptive, illusive shadows of people who had passed through my life and were gone. Their absence left me sidelined and neutral about life. I had not comprehended the effect of their absence, nor had I tried to do so. I had surrendered to absence without investigating its destructive effects on my soul. Now, it wasn't possible to fill the gaps in my life. They had grown and were swallowing me up. I knew this and comprehended that light-years separated me from what was occurring around me, and that I had also come to the point where I was ready to disappear, to be uprooted, to be fully erased.

The same terrifying creatures that had surrounded my brother on the Highway of Death, and before him Saint Anthony in Max Ernst's paintings, were also trying to encircle me. The savage beasts that have no names could scent my loneliness just as they scented blood, and they knew that I had lost the ability to resist. One who is frightened can resist, but one who is lonely has no hope. They had sent me that threatening bullet, not because they knew I would be afraid but because they knew I was alone.

Suddenly I heard the sounds of noisy activity that I knew well. Mamluka seemed to have resumed her activities. I felt relieved. Despite my strong disgust with what she had done, I was fully willing to overlook her sin. Actually, it was the only thing I could do. I was completely incapable of managing the mansion, which was starting to burden and pressure my spirit. She knew every detail—both large and small—within it.

The previous day, everyone had left me after we exchanged kisses that tasted of salty tears and a heavy silence that resembled a death sentence had descended, a cold blue silence that breathed audibly. I understood that they had authorized me to take the last correct decision. Did they actually assume that I knew what was correct?

I decided not to speak with Mamluka about what had occurred and to temporarily avoid the subject to facilitate our dealings with one another. Would she accept this?

I bade her good morning coldly and headed as usual toward the veranda, where Silwan and Guevara were waiting for me. She and I elegantly avoided direct conversation as she served us, but both of us sensed the heavy gray silence that hovered over us.

After breakfast, I sat down with Silwan and listened as he described some of his nightmares. Actually, I was not listening to him, and for the first time, I felt some hatred toward him.

That sudden awful feeling scared me. It was as though I was discovering the hatred I had felt toward him for a long time, ever since he returned from the land of death. I had gathered the twigs of that hatred until they had become ready to be set alight. I even wished he would have a death that would resemble Julnar's disappearance, a death that would entail a great deal of longing, love, and mystery.

I stroked Guevara and felt his warmth and his great love for us. I thought about what I should do as the deadline that the hypocrites had set for us drew closer. To postpone a confrontation with Mamluka, I fled to the large sitting room, which had become my safe haven during those difficult days. I felt very frustrated as I entered it, dragging behind me my guilt at my newly discovered hatred for Silwan and my wish that he would die.

I wanted to escape to something that would divert my thoughts away from that new, shameful feeling. Was there anything to recollect other than the cloudy memory of him, which I had self-indulgently stacked on the highest shelves of memory like a treasure that I would resort to whenever I felt sad or depressed? He was the only one in whose presence I had abandoned all my caution, fear, and hesitation. I had been willing to go with him to the farthest limits, following him like his shadow, just as Julnar had done a long time before, disappearing from our lives forever. She had chosen to disappear with a communist, and I had been willing to disappear with someone who would have been worse to my family—a priest!

Father Faridoun, the pastor who officiated at the Holy Family church and tended it, entered my life like the blade of a sharp knife, slicing it into two equal parts: a before and an after.

At the time, I was in my last year of university studies, and he had begun to make an impact throughout our neighborhood. His exciting arrival and assumption of his sacred duties caused an unusual stir. Stories and gossip about him spread quickly: his firmness, and his ability to attract worshipers to the church, which, before his arrival, had been almost empty except for a few old people. But there it was, full of people during most Mass services and overflowing on Sundays and religious occasions. People even started to speak of miracles that he performed here and there. The popular imagination, full of half-truths and myths, turned him from an ordinary pastor into a popular one. Unlike his predecessors, he no longer only spoke to them of hellfire and seduction by the devil. Instead, he focused on love, mercy, and tolerance. His reputation spread beyond the Christians to the local Muslim community. Everyone was talking about him, and when they did, they would drop their voices and hold their hands in front of their mouths for fear of saying something unworthy of the pastor or that infringed upon his saintly reputation. People are drawn to the sacred, but they also fear it.

The story began when Mary, the cook who had worked for us since the days of my grandfather, the Pasha, asked my mother to relieve her of her tasks because she was old and wanted to return to her birthplace in the north. Her three sons had emigrated and settled abroad, two of them in America and the youngest in Australia.

Mary had a nice house close to our mansion. I knew it well because, as children, we sometimes accompanied her to play with her sons, Touma, Maher, and Nameer. It was made up of two stories and had an open-air Eastern-style courtyard. In its midst was a disused, dried-out fountain, but Mary had turned it into a beautiful spot by planting it with various flowers and plants that gave off a pleasant scent. I was very taken by the design of that charming Baghdadi house, which seemed to me to have sprung out of a mythical tale. After reading the fairy tale of the prince and the frog, I started to enjoy sitting near the fountain, waiting for the ugly frog that would come out of it to turn into a good-looking prince before my eyes, and take me to the heart of the myth.

After the death of Younis, Mary's husband, who had worked for us overseeing maintenance and repairs, Mary lost hope that her sons would return. So she decided to return to the village of Bartala, where she had been born, to die there, since she no longer had any motive to remain in the city that had witnessed her youth, the birth of her children, their departure, and the death of Younis.

The beautiful house had started to suffocate her with its memories, both sweet and bitter, as she put it. Nostalgia beckoned her to return to her roots, to that faraway village, asleep for thousands of years in the Nineveh Plain. She knew that she would eventually be buried in the family cemetery near Younis, and when she described it, her eyes would brim with tears and longing. It was situated on a hill outside the village, and her ancestors and Christian history reposed there.

Mary rejected repeated invitations from her three sons to join them and settle with them in their strange new world, which frightened her. The most she wished for was to see her sons before leaving for her village and dying there so that she could be buried on that hill and become part of the long Christian story in the Land of the Two Rivers. Mary had only two regrets about leaving: the first was parting with my mother, whom she loved. The second was parting with Father Faridoun, the new pastor, "who restored a love for the church among parishioners in the neighborhood, which has become well-known in recent years for its excessive promiscuity," according to Mary. She added, "He's not like the other pastors before him, who encouraged the young to emigrate abroad, to be swallowed up by absence forever" as had happened with her sons. "On the contrary, Father Faridoun is against emigration." That had made him very popular with her and many other Christian mothers, who were unable to leave the land that they had inhabited and loved and were consumed with grief at the departure of their sons to such faraway or cold places. Mary used to talk about him as if he were a saint who had just jumped out of the Bible and was walking and living among us in the Batateen neighborhood.

All that and other talk I had heard about him piqued my curiosity. It seemed like she was talking about the mysterious prince I had long waited for at the edge of the dried-out fountain in her garden. I had awaited his appearance, so that he would ask me to kiss him, liberating him from the curse placed on him by an evil witch, and would then take me away to some unknown place.

When it was time for her to bid me farewell, she drew close to me with a hesitance that she overcame with difficulty, then opened her arms and embraced me. I smelled—between her neck and the edge of her hair that was pulled back into a black scarf—the scent of a history threatened with extinction! I reacted with the same affectionate feelings she was showing. I was unable to abide by the family strictures of not mixing with the other classes, a value we had preserved for generations. This was dear Mary! I embraced her and expressed my genuine affection for her.

She said, "I don't know when I will die, but I hope that I will not be apart from Younis for long. You know that I rejected the idea of selling the house, despite the many tempting offers I received, even though my sons agreed to sell. But I refused and told them I would stay on in the hope that those who were absent would return. If any of them returns, he will find a home awaiting him. They all know how I love you. I have informed them that I will leave the key to the house with you."

She pulled out a key ring to which two keys were attached: one to the front gate and the other to the house. I did not hide my joy at being tasked with this duty. Her house was dear to me as well, and full of beautiful and precious memories. I promised that I would visit it once a week and that I would water the plants and trees that she had planted until God's will was done.

Mary's tale drew my attention to something I had not paid attention to before. The arrival of someone with the status of Father Faridoun in the neighborhood, which had become shared, was not a very important event to us Muslims. But it was very important to the others! Before his arrival, we had never heard a Christian voice among us. They had lived as though they were in a "ghetto." We could hear them speaking the Syriac language and preserving it as though it were what gave them their identity, and they always met everyone with friendly smiles. Things started to change some time after Father Faridoun's arrival, and we began to hear sounds of celebration. Before then, that "ghetto" had been an invisible world to me, although many of them worked for us. Their world was quietly established without noise when the city was established, if not before, and they carefully avoided anything that could provoke the Muslim majority because they realized that patience and circumspection were the best way to keep the Christian presence, which stretched back to pre-Islamic times, from melting into that tumult that no longer accepted diversity.

Father Faridoun, who adhered to Christian values, was of the view that protecting the Christian presence in Iraq depended on being part of society, rather than being segregated from it. The Christian values he believed in were human values that were not exclusive to one category of people. As for faith, it was an individual issue between a believer and what he believed in. Adopting those values was the way to protect Christians in that vibrant neighborhood, where mixing between the religions was familiar and where the borders between the two religions were so narrow that they sometimes became blurred.

Since his words about the common human spirit spread, his name was on every tongue. Even Mamluka became obsessed with Father Faridoun and started bringing news of him to us, or rather to my mother, who had a particular weakness for anything supernatural and sacred. The news of him that she brought mixed fact with myth. Rumors spread that he could perform miracles, was a messenger of virtue, and was stern with deviants, that he inspected small houses and dark corners in bars in search of those who had despaired of salvation, that he bestowed blessings upon everyone until he got to know them one by one. He did not differentiate between Christians and Muslims—he spoke to everyone. Respect mingled with fear, producing a sacred mix, and he was undoubtedly a representative of a divine authority in the Bataween neighborhood.

During the era of the monarchy, the district had been one of the grandest in the capital and had been inhabited by well-known families. But as time went on, it turned into a commercial district that included several of the most famous hotels frequented by people coming from distant and nearby regions because it was close to the capital's medical center on Nasr Street. The clinics and offices of the best-known doctors and lawyers were situated on that street, as well as real estate bureaus and the offices of import and export firms and international airlines. Moreover, it was close to the jolly heart of Baghdad, known as Abu Nuwas Street, which stretched all along the banks of the Tigris River and was home to bars, restaurants, fun fairs, and brothels.

The biggest threat facing the Bataween neighborhood was that many prostitutes and pimps lived there so they could be close to their places of work. So Father Faridoun focused his efforts there. None of his predecessors had managed to make the kind of headway that he had. The priest roamed through all parts of the neighborhood with confident steps day and night. At first, the parishioners he was visiting met him with cold indifference because he had come to change their habits and way of life. But the coldness gradually turned to acceptance, and then to affection, and ended up as something close to sacred veneration.

One cold, foggy morning in January, I left the mansion and headed for the university with some hesitation, because there was no real reason for me to go there that day. I just wanted to get out, rather than staying in the mansion all day. The road was almost empty, except for him. I had never seen him before. Perhaps he was going to tend to a dying woman, to read her some passages he had chosen from the Bible, helping her to overcome her fears and move peacefully into the other world. Our eyes met, and he inclined his head toward me with a gentle smile that I later learned never left his face.

I do not know why I was confused and unable to return his greeting, despite his warm smile that flowed over me. The man was very handsome and attractive, and his face seemed like a natural beauty spot that beckoned one to a stroll! He looked exactly opposite to my preconceived image of him. I did not doubt for a moment that he was the famous priest. Even the neighborhood Muslims had grown to know and respect him, because the need for miracles is not confined to one religion. In my confusion, it was difficult for me to determine his age, but he seemed to be in his late thirties. He was wearing a black robe with a white collar, the way Catholic priests do, and a scarf around his neck with religious symbols all over it. A rather large wooden cross hung from a chain around his neck, and he was not wearing a cap. In his right hand was a bible that he carried close to his heart. He was tall, rather full, and of an athletic build. He had a short beard slightly infiltrated by white, and it matched his short haircut.

He quickly passed by me, leaving behind a lingering whiff of a strange perfume mingled with the scent of church incense and a mysterious, inexplicable trace before being swallowed up by the thick fog. Up till that moment, I had been searching for my sexual identity, which had been unclear because I had repressed it until I could find the right person. I had long been hearing an urgent call emanating from my body, but I had been unable to recognize or define it. In that flash of a moment, it seemed to me as though my body was leading me in spite of myself. It was the eternal call that emanates from women's bodies since the dawn of creation, prompting them to rebel against their minds, which always try to control them.

To be sure, I tried, at the beginning, to repress that call, which surprised me with desires that were out of step with the traditions and customs with which we had been raised at the mansion and which were transformed into the incontrovertible fact that we were different to others.

The fate of Julnar, whose name we never mentioned at our mansion after her departure and permanent erasure from our lives, frightened me to death. I wanted to remain true to the traditions that I had believed in as a life choice, but I felt that my resolve had been shaken. I don't know why seeing him reminded me of the sin, and why Julnar's image became associated with that of Father Faridoun!

The conundrum snowballed in my mind, despite my attempts to ward it off. It was difficult for me to ignore or forget it. Now, I don't know if I had really wanted to or not!

He became a very strong presence at the very heart of my life. I used to listen for news of him from the servants and peasants who worked for us. I had not until then been interested in keeping company with the women who got together in my mother's kitchen in the late morning to have coffee, read their fortunes, and exchange news and secrets. But following that foggy morning, which had left me dizzy, I could not get his image out of my head. To my mother's astonishment, I started to attend those late-morning sessions in the hope that they would mention him in their chatter. Although this usually happened, it was not enough to quench my thirst for him. News of him was always mixed in with exaggeration and tales that I could not possibly believe. This bothered me, and I would think of forgetting him. But I could not.

I hesitated very much and was very frightened of my weakness, but in the end I decided to visit the "holy family" church where he worked, living in the adjoining house. I did not think of justifications for this strange visit but headed for the church as though I were unconscious and unaware of where my destiny was leading me!

I had visited the church before on a few occasions, but I understood that my visit to it this time was completely different. I went to the spot where votive candles were lit by those making vows and special pleas, lit a candle, put it at the feet of the Lady of Sorrows, and made an obscene wish.

The church was empty except for a pathetically thin young woman, wearing black from head to toe. A black embroidered shawl was aesthetically draped on her head. She was kneeling in front of the first row of seats, very close to the statue of

Christ crucified upon the cross. She was speaking to him in a low voice that she slightly raised at times, but her words remained unclear and only intelligible to the two of them. She did not look straight at him, but held her head slightly turned to the side, either out of respect or fear, I could not make out which.

Her hands were clasped in front of her bosom, and a rosary with agate beads and a golden cross at the end of it dangled from them. The girl seemed as though she wanted to catch a shadow or a soul, or maybe she was searching for hope.

Not far from her, a rather plump lady flitted about like a bee as she carried out her daily cleaning chores, her gaze shifting between me and the girl wrapped in black. Perhaps she feared the girl would melt and vanish out of piety before Christ bleeding on the cross. After she saw me lighting a candle to the Virgin, she stopped moving around and started to look straight at me with a boldness tinged with some caution. She definitely knew everyone who came to the church. I felt slightly disconcerted, because the last thing I wanted was to speak with someone I did not know. So I remained standing before the Virgin's statue, not quite knowing what I was doing there.

The soothing cool, and gentle dimness seduced me into sitting not far from the thin girl and to enjoy that strange calmness that insulated me from the disturbing chaos on the surrounding streets. I began to study the walls of the church, which were full of primitive paintings that betrayed the amateurishness and lack of talent of their creators. But the religious awe that their chosen subjects inspired was moving. The artists had chosen to focus on the sad hour of the crucifixion as it was related in the Bible. It seemed to me that combining the Bible account of it with painting prompted the observer to sympathize with the paintings, irrespective of their artistic value, which had not been the artist's main concern. But because I had studied art, I could not ignore their primitiveness, which bewildered and troubled me. The church was dark, even though the sun shone brightly outside. It also had a slight musty smell that mingled with Omani incense—and the scent of a man I had come to search for.

The pale light that seeped into the middle of the church through its dusty windows spread an atmosphere of sadness that stuck to the body. It seemed as though the plump lady had not cleaned the windows for a long time. The old wooden seats were dark brown, but the parts of them on which people sat had turned to light brown, as though every believer who sat on them had come away with a bit of their color, leaving an indelible trace. How many people had sat there listening to priests' sermons and speeches of priests, harboring their fears, wishes, boredom, or piety, desires for a divine miracle and their sins which they had brought here in the hope of finding salvation. And many other things.

I sensed all this, and that feeling gave me a strange enjoyment, and my heart told me that my visit would not be the last.

I repeatedly visited the church when it was empty of worshippers. It was normal that a kind of friendly relationship should spring up between me and the cleaning lady. Once I introduced myself and she heard my family name, her look of suspicion disappeared. I learned from her the husband of the thin girl who always wore black had emigrated to Denmark three years earlier and she had not had any word from him. She came to pray every day, to beg that his fate had not been the same as many young immigrants whose dreams had been buried at sea.

My visits to the church were motivated by a wish that resembled that of a mischievous jinni living deep inside me, dancing with incredible daintiness, tickling me and promising me a meeting with him, despite my guilt, which would not allow me to easily act on my madness. His shadow had remained with me since that foggy day, pushing me toward recklessness and an abandonment of all the ideas I had been brought up with, which were in stark contradiction with my foolhardy impulse.

What was the secret behind it? Was it the myths that were spun around him and spread through the streets of Bataween or within its half-darkened apartments, its bars, its miserable corners, and the mansions of the rich?

Had his handsome looks dazzled me as I beheld the most beautiful of Baghdad mornings in his face? In fact, it was not important to me to know why I wanted to see him. What mattered was that I did. Chasing his shadow had begun to bring me happiness, pleasure, and an addiction to something I had not known before. More importantly, I had shaken off the boredom that had dominated my life at the time.

Mamluka, who spent most of her time at the mansion, would disappear at noon, and no one knew where she went. My mother certainly knew about it. As for us, we didn't care.

On returning in the afternoon, she would sit with my mother in the kitchen, "the kingdom of secrets" to prepare afternoon tea and sandwiches, which we enjoyed taking at that time of day, and she would report the latest neighborhood news and developments since the previous day to my mother.

Sometimes I would go into the kitchen to fetch something, and they would stop their whispered conversation. Mamluka was and remained the source of all the news that came to the mansion through its back doors. It was the kind of news that was improper to openly talk about. She knew a lot of tales that were in circulation during those days about the personality that had thrust itself into the neighborhood and captured the popular imagination in it. By coincidence, I overheard them one day talking about an illegitimate relationship that Father Faridoun was having with a young girl.

Irrespective of whether the news was accurate or not, a sudden feeling of jealousy attacked me, like an animal that had been stalking its prey in the dark. Yes, a burning jealousy that coursed within me like fire, and I didn't know how to extinguish or control it. I had seen him only once, and fleetingly at that, and I hadn't even returned his greeting.

I decided that I ought to put my increasingly agitated feelings to the test. I could not keep going to the church in the hope of seeing him and get swallowed up instead by the avid gossip of the cleaning lady, Esther. The last time, after despairing of her sense of initiative, I had drawn her attention to the dust that had accumulated on the windows, preventing the sunlight from entering the church, and she had cleaned them so well that they looked as though the glass had just been installed.

Although I had made a decision, it remained vague, and I needed to determine the course of the adventure I had decided to embark upon, which had begun to change the pattern of my life. I began to keep myself to myself, drowning myself in daydreaming at Mary's house.

I visited Mary's house once a week to keep the promise I had made her to water the plants and take care of them. Eventually, I began to spend my time daydreaming and neglected to water the plants, so I enlisted the help the prostitute Regina, who was Mary's neighbor.

I knew that Regina was practicing the oldest profession in the world, but no one mentioned it openly. It was only referred to in whispers and hints. After her youth had passed, she would help Mary to clean the house and keep it presentable. So it was logical that I should run into Regina every time I visited the house.

My relationship with Regina started out as formal and cold. She would come to help me whenever she saw me going into the house. We would exchange a few words, but I remained cautious, cutting short the conversation whenever I sensed that it might extend to personal matters, because her reputation did not appeal to me. But as time when by, I discovered that she had a sense of fun and humor, and that this was one of her natural talents. She was clearly good-hearted, despite the vulgarity of some of her language. Eventually, her vulgarity made me laugh hard, rendering our short interactions enjoyable.

I did not imagine Father Faridoun to be a saint, so my admiration for her grew when I found out that she was one of the few people who had rebelled against the pastor's power. Regina said she had not been to church for a long time. Because she needed spiritual blessing, she set up something of a small altar in her apartment. In the middle of it stood an icon of the Virgin Mary, whom she always described as her only friend in the cruel world that had shown her no mercy.

At first, I was actually scared of talking to her for fear that the sins she had committed by practicing prostitution for many years would stick to me. But I gradually discovered that she was loyal to her old neighbor, Mary, and was at peace with herself despite her heavy burden of sin. Regina did not believe that Father Faridoun was not having sex with a woman. She would say, "I can tell what a man is like by his eyes, and the pastor's eyes say a lot, and it's different to what people say about him."

I wanted to believe her irrespective of how valid her argument was. Her words held hope, which remained within the realm of doubt, and I wanted to move it to the realm of certainty.

Not only did Regina have a bitter sense of humor. She was also addicted to alcohol, and liked to sing. She only performed the old classical songs, and she was very good at it. She liked to look back, and she considered everything in the past to be pure. We saw eye to eye on this view. I wondered which past she was talking about. I spoke of a past to which I was proud to belong, but I didn't quite know what Regina meant by referring to the past. It seemed to me that she was nostalgic for a time when she used to control men!

Her voice was full of sweet sorrow. When she sang, her features softened, and she practiced the art of enjoying words, articulating through lips besmirched with the remains of cheap lipstick and alcohol with great feeling and passion.

The trust between us grew, and I gave her a copy of the key to Mary's house, so she could do the necessary tasks when I couldn't spare the time. Our relationship strengthened smoothly, to my amazement, as I searched futilely for a reasonable cause for me to keep company with such a creature. But I could only find a superficial justification, which was that I wanted to escape my own skin into which I had been placed by my family and its ancient history. She didn't know who I was, was completely ignorant of my family's history, had not thought that Mary would be friends with upper-class people, and was totally uninterested in lineage. She had known all sorts of men and found such matters very complicated and trivial.

Regina and I agreed to meet one lovely spring evening in Mary's garden and that she would prepare an appetizing meal, which I knew she was very good at. When I opened the garden gate, I was surprised to find that she had placed the table next to the abandoned well, the edges of which were decorated by the flowers that I carefully tended. It was a beautiful, even captivating scene, and it set me completely at ease as I shut the green iron gate behind me. In that place, I was no longer myself, I didn't belong to my history, which I had left outside the gate. I turned into nothing more than a woman who had come in search of something exotic that would banish the boredom that had taken hold of her life, even for a single spring evening. Regina had prepared the appetizers, and placed the locally made arrack bottle in the middle of the table. Her philosophy included drinking several glasses before dinner as aperitifs.

I did not want to drink alcohol, but I decided to put a glass in front of me and to sip a little bit from it so as not to spoil her enjoyment. Regina liked to divide the bottle into four equal quarters. The first loosened her tongue, so that she kept telling jokes and prattling merrily, which was the best thing to happen to her during her day. The second quarter made her lighter on her feet, prompting her to dance and sway to the tunes of a small recorder that she would bring with her and place at the edge of the well. It incessantly played very old Iraqi songs, which I also enjoyed listening to. The third, which she usually never finished, opened the floodgates of sorrow and bitter memories, and she would bewail her bad luck, which had turned her into the talk of the neighborhood. She would accuse the inhabitants of ingratitude and other negative attributes and consider herself more virtuous and moral than most of them, since she knew all their secrets. But she would quickly reaffirm that she could not move away from them and live elsewhere, which amounted to a kind of psychological punishment and continuous self-flagellation. The one thing she would not talk about in detail, however drunk she got, was Father Faridoun.

When I brought him up in the hope of finding out more about him, she would sober up slightly and her speech would become more restrained, repeating what others said about him. When I questioned her more persistently or asked her why she didn't go to church, and why she said he had a relationship with a young girl, she would avoid answering me, either by crying or by singing drunkenly, strangely snapping her fingers as though they were a musical instrument.

I remained conscious of the fact that I was going along a very dangerous path, one that was probably more dangerous than the one that Julnar had chosen. I could not imagine my mother's reaction had she found out that I was keeping company with Regina, a creature whose company I enjoyed, and whom they regarded as abominable. But I also knew that I was no longer able to stop the train of my fate, which I could clearly see was leading me toward a bottomless pit. I only hoped that I would meet him at the end of the journey, even if he were the last person I would see.

Regina had not been to church since her childhood, because she was in eternal disagreement with the church. But she knew all the news surrounding it. She once told me that she had heard from a woman she trusted that the pastor had referred to her in his Sunday sermon without mentioning her by name, simply referring to a prostitute who had disobeyed God. Regina took it personally and decided that he had been nasty to her. I tried to convince her otherwise, pointing out that she wasn't the only prostitute in the Bataween neighborhood. But she was insistent, and it even seemed to me as though she wanted to be that sinful woman, as though she had a deeply rooted desire to torture herself.

My strange friendship with her began to take on some fixed rituals. I was a creature of habit and ritual, from which I did not deviate in my relationship with Regina.

We began to meet on a weekly basis at Mary's house. I would give her money to shop and prepare a small feast that included a bottle of local arrack. She preferred its taste to any other alcohol. I fell into the habit of drinking lightly with her. Although I did this hesitantly and nervously, the drink's sharp odor and the atmosphere of our get-together were enough to transport me to an atmosphere of pleasant liberation that she would make available to me. The garrulous prostitute was lonely, although she had many relatives in the neighborhood and knew most of its inhabitants.

Her good looks had not completely abandoned her, and she still had an attractive appearance that she was proud of, especially when she was sober and freshened up her tired face with light makeup.

Early on in our relationship, I totally avoided talking to her about the details of her body-selling trade, although she was aware that I knew about it. Both of us avoided mentioning the subject, even when she was completely seized by drunkenness after consuming half a bottle of arrack. I had clearly drawn a red line between us and broaching that subject, and she did not approach it because she wanted to hold on to her relationship with me. Actually, I didn't know why she was keen to keep up her relationship with someone as boring as me.

I began to get addicted to her tales, which were full of a lasciviousness and exoticness that I was not used to and had not even heard of before. The enjoyment prompted me to allow her to cross my red lines, and I cautiously asked her some questions to facilitate her delving into the hidden world I knew nothing about, except what I had read in books or seen on TV or at the cinema—the world of prostitution.

I thought I had hurt her feelings when I asked her once,

"How can you bear to sleep with a different man you don't know every day?" She laughed lightly as though I had told her a joke. Then she started to reveal some details, and I found that they were attractive to me. I eventually got hooked on such obscene talk, and I even asked more intimate questions, enjoying my foray into that verbal filth, which did not pertain to me, but by coincidence to the woman who was sitting beside me.

She was not embarrassed by what she was telling me. On the contrary, I sensed in her a kind of indifference that bordered on habit and a familiarity with suppressing worrying questions, that perhaps went as far as actually enjoying the job itself.

She related the details to me comically, causing me to alternate between wanting to laugh openly and secretly wishing that I could trade places with her. I got to the point where I enjoyed pretending to be her after our meetings ended. I would think of the details of her day and practice the dream of my own prostitution on my empty bed with my imagination aflame.

It then became normal for her to use obscene language in front of me and to call things by their names without embarrassment, and I encouraged it. At first, I couldn't stop myself from blushing, but in the end I wanted to hear more of the obscene words I had never heard all my life.

My amazement at discovering a world that had maps that had been unfamiliar to me before, even though I was just doing so through listening to metaphoric descriptions, became more important than anything else at the time. To her, having sex was a very ordinary thing that all humans experienced, and perhaps it was the nicest thing in life. With an arrogance that went beyond self-confidence, she said, "Everyone engages in legal prostitution when they go home." I discovered from Regina that the atmosphere of *A Thousand and One Nights* was not limited to the world of books and oral tradition, but that it still lived among us, even if we were unable to sense it or believed it did not exist, perhaps because we didn't want to know anything about it. The rumblings of those nights had continued uninterrupted among us for hundreds of years along the banks of the Wise Tigris, its running waters washing the sinful and the virtuous alike.

Yes, I grew fond of that creature, who spoke to me about her life without any embarrassment and perhaps with a bit of nostalgia for a lost virtue, an invisible thread of sadness, or a desire to jump from the top of the Eiffel Tower. A woman who did not compare herself to other women, not out of shame or a sense of superiority but out of a sense of her own individuality and the limits of her cold isolation.

She seemed keen on her strange relationship with me because, as it seemed to me, it gave her a rare opportunity to have a relationship with that world that she could never become reconciled with, a world she had left a long time ago, but still yearned for: the world of virtue.

Regina was not a bad woman at all. She helped others without forcing them to ask for her help. At the same time, she accepted their ingratitude, which was part of the game of coexistence of two opposed values in the same pace—virtue and sin.

Strangely, she never asked me any personal questions, even after I had invaded her life with questions of my own, and even after she had consumed the third, dangerous quarter of a bottle of arrack, at which point, her inhibitions would dissipate at the edges of the glass from which she was drinking. In the end, the empty bottle would come to rest on some grassy spot in Mary the cook's garden.

Our relationship bestowed a temptingly magical freedom on me that could have taken another, completely unexpected direction. One day, my right shoulder and neck were tense and painful. Regina cautiously asked me to take off my blouse, then produced a strange-smelling, pungent Chinese-made oil in a small bottle that had an axe drawn on its label. She poured a few drops onto her palms and then started massaging me with hands, trained to touch pleasure spots. At first, I was disturbed by the feel of the oil and the strange hands on my flesh, which gradually absorbed the heat of the oil. I began to feel it quickly spreading all over my body, even in the folds of my mind. Her hand went round and round, and I lost the ability to concentrate and was overcome by a desire to completely surrender, as though I had been overcome by a pleasurable, anesthetizing daze that was new to my body.

Hands have a clear language, and the language of her hand had a clear message that was inviting me to stop resisting. I felt her breath as her face drew close to my shoulder and neck, and I almost fainted. Long after, I was never able to know if that signified a deeply buried desire to respond to her trained hand, or whether it was something else deeply buried within me. At the end of that brief adventure, I was able to pull up my blouse with difficulty to cover my naked shoulder. My flesh bore her hand marks, and her breath infiltrated me mercilessly. It was a strange feeling that promised freedom from the slavery to which I had voluntarily become a prisoner, or to which my family had subjected me because we were the bearers of a message of civilization in a society that was breaking down. It was a feeling that promised me a quick escape from within the strictures of a taboo that we had inherited ever since our family had begun to value its social status at the expense of its members freedom—that is, for seven generations, according to the family tree that we kept at the mansion, as though it were a holy statue or a taboo upon the walls of which the dust of hundreds of years had gathered, and which Regina's trained hand had almost wiped away in seconds.

There was no denying that getting closer to her turned me into a more aware and daring person, even a more cheerful one! I felt that I was being liberated from something idiotic that I could not name. I had never before imagined the existence of such a vast, profligate, firm, and exciting world that had enriched my vocabulary. The world in which I had grown up had stubbornly denied the very existence of such creatures, and it was shameful to even think about them or believe in them. But Regina proved to me the existence of that world—its men, women, and illegitimate children; its epics, heroes, aesthetic myths, and its primitiveness that had freed itself of the burden of history. People living among us, thronging the alleys of the city that denied their existence for fear of a false reputation and a fraudulent shame. A world filled with epic tales and captivating love stories, and some of its names provoked terror in the upper and lower worlds.

No one wanted to awaken that cursed, magical world for fear of the volatile scandals that would surely affect many families and persons in the upper world of the heterogenous city. I discovered my weakness compared to Regina's strength. She was not conscious of her limits and perceived this as natural.

Regina was someone outside all the contexts I had experienced with the ordinary people I had known. She was unique and had superpowers that she deliberately wasted. She knew very well that she could have achieved more for herself than what life had given her, but she did not want to leave the mud to which she had become accustomed. On more than one occasion, she surprised me with a natural gesture, behaving in a lovely and refined manner that led me to believe that she came from the best of families. There were times when she was wise and flexible, and I once caught sight of her in a moment of noble silence. I liked to watch her smoke. Holding a cigarette between her fingers, she looked like a beautiful painting by an anonymous artist, the tips of her fingers touching her forehead when she was deep in thought, then looking at me scornfully from the corner of her eye, as if to say, "You're naïve."

Was I attracted to her because I wanted to imagine my relationship to the departed Julnar, leaving me with a burning desire to get to know her?

I knew I was merging the two women. But I was doing that very consciously, the way I had learned to mix colors in my artistic studies. She made me feel as though childhood had not quite left me yet.

I seemed to her like someone completely different from an educational, cultural, social, and religious perspective, someone to whom she could disclose things that she could not to others who belonged to her world, and it was something she had not experienced. Even her relationship with Mary had not gone beyond the limits of neighborliness, and it was a cautious relationship, despite the affection they had for each other. Mary had only opened her home to her after her three sons had emigrated and her husband, Younes, had died. For many years before that, Regina had simply smiled and greeted Mary.

I undoubtedly tried to stop myself from completely plunging into that strange relationship. I tried to reimpose limits on it whenever I felt that I had gone too far, like the time I had allowed her to touch my taut shoulder. I did not want to ask her why she had resorted to prostitution as a profession, even though she was a smart and beautiful woman who could have made something else of her life before slipping into that world that never forgave anyone who abandoned it.

But one long hot summer evening when the moon was full, she decided of her own accord to talk. That evening, she opted to tell me about her journey to the other bank, like the goddess Ishtar, who had descended to the underworld to search for her lover, Tammuz. I did not want to interrupt her because I sensed her strong desire to vent, and it pleased me. That evening, she finished her second glass of arrack and banged it onto the table.

It had all begun when her family was forced to emigrate from the north to the capital in search of better opportunities, which were nonexistent in the cold, rugged mountains that were in a perpetual state of ethnic no-war, no-peace. Her father worked at a hotel owned by a relative, near their home.

Her drunken father would return home late every night, and the "torture party," as she referred to it, would begin. He would beat and curse her mother, but he stayed away from Regina and her young siblings. Then she understood that she was the reason for the torture borne by her mother. Her father wanted her to work at the same hotel where he worked, and her mother objected strongly because she feared the fate that awaited her daughter if she worked at that shady hotel.

"My mother used to cry all day because she understood the limits of her ability to stop the inevitable catastrophe that was coming sooner or later. All she could do was to postpone it," said Regina.

Regina was a pretty sixteen-year-old at the time, and she would overhear that unbearable arguing every night when her drunk father came home until she gradually became psychologically prepared to do anything to break out of that demonic circle.

Smiling sarcastically, she told me that she had inherited her taste for drinking arrack from her father, who got drunk every evening with the hotel owner, Saman, who persisted in asking when his daughter would start work at the hotel.

Saman could not marry Regina because he was already married. He and his wife quarreled all the time. He would direct a torrent of curses at her and threaten to convert to Islam to subdue her and satisfy his sexual desires, which she refused to indulge because of his drunkenness and because, from her devout perspective, he was spending his money in an ungodly way.

Every day, Saman reassured Regina's father that he would

treat her like a queen if he could convince her to work at the hotel.

"My father was not unaware of Saman's motives, but he also was powerless and overwhelmed by the debts he owed Saman, who used to make him sign documents every time he borrowed."

Her mother's strong resistance did not persist indefinitely. No one could hold back Regina's fate. The pressures were stronger than everyone. It all happened quickly.

Regina said, "That night, my father didn't come home. He came in the morning as I was getting ready to go to school, and he was very drunk. He told me, 'You won't be going to school today.' I understood why, and I wanted to end the problem. I knew he would be taking me to my new place. As I walked with him, we didn't exchange a single word."

She said that she suddenly felt she had grown up, skipping some years, and she realized that she would never again go to the school that she loved. She matured very quickly in the heat of the blazing sun, the smell of alcohol that wafted from him and obscured the scent of fatherhood, his unseen tears, his shaking hand as he strongly gripped her wrist, his eyes brimming with shame and surrender, and the shaky silence between them. He did not sleep at home that night either, and it was a lovely evening without his beatings and curses.

"We all wished he would stay away forever," she whispered.

But she was not exclusively restricted to Saman's bed for long, rolling out of it after a short while into other beds, including that of Khalil, Saman's son, with whom she fell in love and by whom she became pregnant.

As she related to me that great amount of private detail, full of humiliation and oppression, I couldn't stop myself from comparing the two of us in a cold, neutral way, devoid of emotion. I compared my calm, glaringly boring life to her stormy, boisterous life that seemed like a boat that had been cruelly and violently tossed into a stormy sea with no lifesaving means on board.

How could she have borne all that? How was she able to relate to a stranger like me all those intimate details that had been molded by oppression? Her powerful presence before me shook my life, my convictions, and all that I had believed to be constant. A fateful game by unseen fingers. What if I had been in her place, and she in mine? How would both our stories have changed?

I wanted to flee from her presence, to stop her from narrating as she swallowed glasses of arrack and enjoyed sucking on a salty olive. She began to sing, and I got an even stronger sense of her pain as it crept into me from all directions. Her rich, passionate voice expressed her pain with a refinement that made feel comfortable and gave me a vague feeling of oppression.

I suddenly got up like someone who had just felt the sting of a scorpion, and said with an impoliteness that she immediately sensed, "I must go now."

She put her glass down gently on the table after she had stopped singing, and her words threw me an unexpected challenge. "You're the one who provoked all that pain with your deliberate silence."

I needed several days to digest all that had been said

that evening. It left me with nothing more than a feeling of anxiety that violently oscillated between disgust and sympathy with that confusing creature, who seemed to bear no kind of hatred to any being, even toward her father. When she spoke of him, it seemed as though she were searching for justifications for his heinous act, and that angered me. I was, after all, the descendent of a high-born family and had learned to sculpt hatred and to turn it into a lethal weapon that I threw at everyone to confront the vulgarity prevailing around me. I would use it to block out anything that was inconsistent with my beliefs. How could she rise above a superior feeling like hatred? Was she trying to tell me that she was better than me? Who was she?

The dry plants that were almost rigid around the well in Mary's garden told me that she had not been there in my absence. I could not deny that during the five days when I did not see her, I missed her humorous, uninhibited talk, which was free of all limitations that constrained me. I missed her merry spirit, the wise way in which she philosophized issues despite the simplicity of her words, the consummate way in which she gossiped, the way in which she held her cigarette and sucked in her breath after drinking a sip of arrack. I missed her adept way of preparing delicious mezza dishes, and her assertion every time she laid the table that the eye relishes a meal before the mouth. I missed her attractive, distinctive scent, her resonant laugh that was often accompanied by a coughing fit caused by her heavy smoking. I thought a lot about her tolerance toward her father, who had been found dead at an illegal bar. She had sent his body to the village of

Batoufa amid the distant high mountains in the very north of the country.

All of that prompted me to think about visiting her to apologize, but visiting the home of a known prostitute was a problem. What would the people who saw me entering her house say?

On my way to her, a bothersome question that I was unprepared to handle nagged at me: Where was this extraordinary relationship, which made me feel that I was committing a sin by persisting in it, leading me? I missed her but could not seriously consider her to be my friend. For starters, that notion filled me with disgust for myself.

My unfathomable wish to draw closer to Father Faridoun turned into a ball of fire that threatened to set fire to my whole life. Being close to her made it easier for me to bear the vague waiting. With her, I was a woman with no history, no well-known name, no mores and traditions to encumber me, without anything—just a woman searching for her happiness in a desert that I did not know how to leave...and she, Regina, was my only guide in that world.

At sunset, when the outline of things takes on the mysteriousness and deceptiveness of darkness, I saw the light in her flat and I entered the building. Its entrance was saturated with the smell of urine. The depressing pale light intensified sense of alienation from the whole world. I continued to walk upstairs, but my ascension felt more like a descent. The edges of the stairs were chipped away, and what remained of my logic was aggressively calling on me to back down.

At last, here was the door of her flat, which bore traces

of old kicks and holes, although it had not been completely destroyed. That was almost certainly a side of the life she lived that she had not yet told me about. There were also unintelligible chalk scribblings by badly behaved children on the door, and a small colored sticker depicting the Virgin Mary. The smell of fried eggplant wafted out from behind the closed door. Abandoned furniture and other things I couldn't make out stood in the hallway separating the three flats that shared the second floor. I hesitantly knocked at the door, which had no name or any other signs on it to indicate it was hers.

The door opened, and Regina appeared from behind it, smiling in an unfamiliar way. She was heavily made up, prompting me to ask her if she were going out. She shook her head and looked at me with a cheek that did not stop her from opening the dilapidated door more widely to make it easier for me to enter the prostitute's den.

"Are you hungry?" she asked in spontaneous way that suited her exclusively. The smell of fried eggplants did not disguise a moldy odor that had taken root in the flat, which saw no sun. Inside the home of the prostitute who was known throughout the neighborhood, I was surprised by the large number of pictures and stickers—in different sizes, shapes, and colors—of the famous Eiffel Tower. Unable to contain my curiosity, I asked about that. She tossed her head with a childish spontaneity and said, "I don't know."

She had no answer, even as she stood there dazzled and delighted by all those pictures. She surveyed them with a deep-seated wonder. "One day, I will travel over there, and I will go up to the top of the tower, once I am rid of my love for the Bataween neighborhood, which sticks to me like the curse of a church," she said with her back turned to me, as she turned over the eggplants. Deep down, I felt an urge to hug her, to be kind to her and say something that matched that sort of situation. But the rest of the traditions I had been raised to observe stopped me, so I strongly repressed my emotions.

I felt that I was not free, and that dozens of invisible eyes were watching me all the time. Regina said she had not left the neighborhood for forty-four years, except when circumstances that could not be postponed required her to, which in her dictionary that I was familiar with, meant death.

Her mother's death, the death of her brother in the same desert oil war in which my brother Silwan lost his sanity—she buried them there, in that faraway village, and returned home. The disclosure that Regina became used to practicing with me helped me to allow her free rein when speaking, even when she used words that violated public decency. I deliberately suspended anything that might limit her verbal flow, which I loved, and which allowed me to delve with her into her unique magic world. I thought about enlisting her help to get closer to the person whose shadow had prompted me to enter a world to which I was a stranger, particularly, since she was considered one of the neighborhood's most important secret keys and knew its inside secrets, although I had inhabited the same neighborhood since birth.

Perhaps she had a way of making it easier for me to slip into the holiest sanctum of the person whose image had taken me over, lived within me and refused to leave. And even if she couldn't do anything, just talking about it would assuage the anguish that used to overcome me…maybe!

One day, I returned from university and went straight to Mary's house without passing by the mansion. I found her waiting for me, as we had arranged an appointment. She had prepared everything to make our hours together distinctive and pleasant. "My friend the prostitute," I thought to myself and smiled. She noticed my smile and asked me about the secret that I couldn't tell her about.

What game had I become mixed up in? When would that mischievous jinni within me stop? Who was I? What was I doing there? Which of the two worlds was closer to my soul, the world of age-old ancient traditions or those lovely secret sessions that I couldn't tell anyone about? Regina put her hand over her mouth and whispered the latest dirty jokes in my ear, her eyes glancing here and there like someone watching a ghost who might have passed nearby.

During that meeting, I wanted to keep up with her drinking as I wrestled with the idea of confessing. At first, she opened her eyes wide in delight as she poured out more of the intoxicating fluid for me. But I was careful not to lose control of my mind and my tongue, although my speech began to slur. Once those glasses that I had consumed helped me to muster the courage I usually lacked, I said, "Regina, I'm in love with Father Faridoun."

She looked at me in strange silence. I was unable to decipher that look, which hurt me slightly, because it implied some disapproval. She drank from the tip of her glass and didn't look at me. She looked instead toward the abandoned well where we used to sit as though I were not there. I was overcome by an overwhelming feeling of embarrassment and cheapness. My blushing face exposed me before her. I had never imagined that finding my way to the path I had decided to take would push me to such depths of cheapness. Nevertheless, I felt no desire to back down. What cheek!

I don't know how much time elapsed as we remained in that strange state of silent communication until she got up and left everything to go to her apartment in the adjacent building, leaving me alone to drown in a silence that stuck to me and gradually began to transform into a shameful scandal, because I had disclosed what could not be disclosed.

During that damned night, I got no sleep. I wished that I could erase her from my life and forget about her, that I could forgo forever my crazy desire, which had led me in spite of myself, without any self-respect or any trace of the dignity of which I had been proud, to run after the first person who had passed by and left me with a ball of fire.

It wasn't Regina's unexpected reaction that pained me. What really worried me was the power that had taken hold of me and forced me to change the course of my life, and to enter voluntarily into a strange world in which I found myself floundering without any knowledge or planning.

When Regina had fallen pregnant by Khalil, the hotel owner's son, many years previously, they brought in a licensed midwife to help her to abort the child. Following the procedure, the fetus was buried beneath the lemon tree in the hotel garden. The day I learned this, I knew how far her limits would stretch, and I was careful not to breach them. She had never consumed lemons since her abortion. Where were my limits?

Her dearest wish was to go to the top of the Eiffel Tower while drunk one day. But what did I wish for?

I stopped writing and delving deep into those memories. I was in the large sitting room sitting before Max Liebermann's painting of Samson and Delilah, which embodies the meanings of love, deception, betrayal, and arrogance. Samson, the hero with legendary strength, whose love for Delilah caused him to overlook necessary caution and to give her all his secrets. She understood how to vanquish him once she learned his weak point, which he had disclosed to her in a moment of weakness. She cut his hair, causing him to lose his great gift forever.

At first glance, the painting gives the impression that the artist wanted to capture the moment of Delilah' victory and to convict her by catching her committing the act of betrayal. However, the painting is deeper than that flimsy surface. They are naked on a bed with white sheets. Samson is collapsed on her legs as though begging her, or as though he did not want to see the betrayal of the woman he loved, declaring his final painful surrender. It might even be said that he appears to be a humble supplicant as she gently puts her left hand on his head, perhaps with contempt. She is actually pushing his head downward, as if saying, "You aren't what you used to be."

In her right hand, she holds up the hair she has deceitfully cut from his head, turning him into an ordinary person. She stretches her neck upward, toward the distance, to the utmost limits of betrayal, oblivious of his anguish, his pain, or his fate. Her lips bear a rancorously joyous smile. Perhaps she is shouting and saying, "Come, all you traitors of the world. None of you have reached the limit that I have." Because it is a historic betrayal, the artist has depicted her naked body as flabby, presenting her as a woman suddenly growing old in the flush of victory. Was the artist acting punitively? Was he telling us that betrayal, whatever its justifications, is the lowest of vices? Could Delilah be an alternate Eve, who seduced Adam and brought him down from paradise? No, there was a big difference between seduction and betrayal.

I felt the presence of my grandfather, always starting debates on philosophical issues.

At the far right of the painting, a hand emerges from the darkness. Delilah delivers Samson to his enemies. Is that what I did to Father Faridoun? Did I not strip him of the halo he had had before he met me? Oh, why did I want to write about all that now, and for whom? Maybe for him and for me. With him, I was possessed by a state of crazy impulsiveness that turned me into someone able to transcend all the boundaries that were forbidden by a hypocritical society that assumed a shallow and false moral superiority, the boundaries that separated religions and sects and defined the separate spheres allocated to men and to women, the boundaries of ingratitude, mutiny, looseness, and indifference. As I carried his image deep within me like a precious treasure, I was no longer able to distinguish the limits of all those mythical boundaries, and I went beyond them.

Regina was able to put me in touch with him. She was adept at playing that field and accessing its secrets. I didn't ask her how she had accomplished that, because I wanted to

avoid humiliating myself in front of her again. I didn't want
to look into her eyes, which flashed with questions ranging
from condemnation to accusations of deception and other
damned things that I could not decipher. I also knew that our
relationship had ended the day I met with Father Faridoun,
and I didn't regret it. I did not know how it all happened. He
and I did not exchange trivial questions. We did not have the
idle luxury of asking. We both wanted to overstep the mud of
trivial words and meaningless questions.

When Regina told me that Father Faridoun wanted to
get to know me, I smiled in a way I had never done before.
As I looked in the mirror, I was amazed. I felt that my smile
resembled Delilah's smile as she delivered Samson to his
enemies. As my smile widened to occupy the whole mirror, I
realized that the secret source of his strength was within my
grasp: his sacred halo!

The sweet scent of intoxicating Omani incense hung outside the entrance to his home, settling at the tip of my tongue.
It mingled with the scent of walls that supported shelves full
of books that were full of heroism, sacrifice, pain, and the scent
of missing pleasure, which was mine.

I had to first pass through the long corridor, with its walls
full of paintings and photographs of all the priests who had
served the church since its establishment. I avoided looking at
them as I passed beneath their gazes, which were either for-
bidding or lecherous. Many of the icons, pictures, and crosses
hanging on the walls were gifts from the devout and from
penitents and supplicants of divine forgiveness. But I was an
accomplice of sin, which I pushed toward the dark depths,

linked with many frightening questions, throwing heavy weights on top of them, and immobilizing them with locks that had preserved secrecy since the beginning of creation. Of one glaring thing I was sure. I was fully conscious of my sin and willing to pay the necessary price! On his large soft bed, covered by the same white sheets that covered Samson and Delilah's bed in the painting, we could hear the noise from the adjacent street, and it sounded chaotic. That moment, I knew I would not forget him, and that he would stick to me like the prompting of a cunning demon.

Feelings, anticipation, dread, yearning, and waiting all merged to reveal the vast dimensions of the body I had carried for so long, as though I had only been holding it in trust for him.

As time went by, a quietness would seep into the room, pushing away the noise to faraway places. I would listen to my breath and his, to the rustle of clothes being removed from bodies to the language of eyes brimming with a desire too great to be expressed by words, to the language of fingertips, to thoughts that chuckled audibly, to feelings that turned into tangible material things. I knew that he felt the same way about me as I did about him. I was the last surface upon which that beautiful holy bird had alighted. I was seduction, I was love, I was the curse that could not be cast off. I began to understand how that beautiful creature in my hand pulsated. It was with him that I felt liberated and light-spirited, experiencing a deep longing to transcend the boundaries that had previously scared me.

Every time I left his bed, I wondered where all those

unsettled feelings that eagerly searched for something with a dazzling immediacy came from. It seemed like soap bubbles, beautiful, wonderful, with captivating colors and lasting only moments. Neither of us had distinctive sexual skills, and we were like two children tripping across the bed with joy.

The relationship was clear and equal from the beginning. We kept it well removed from the boring, monotonous definitions that others used cheaply. Both of us understood the dimensions and danger of the adventure we had embarked upon. We avoided talking because talk was a limited way of communication. Longing, passion, addiction to one another, our feeling that we were stretching out on an impossible bed, all of that brought us together. Neither of us considered crossing over onto the other's space, so the passionate relationship we had concealed by silence and sin continued. It was a state closer to a conspiracy than to love. For a year and a half, I was the happiest person in a city that had come to hate anyone who was happy.

I remained watchful with a mysterious, faceless anxiety that welled up from deep within, or perhaps it had been lurking there from the beginning. It was something that had feelings I could not understand. Could this be love? Was I able to go further than I had already managed to go? I gave him my body without hesitation or regret, and the strict secrecy that we observed to guard the longevity of our passionate relationship limited such negative feelings. No one knew about us, except for her, who had brokered our love: Regina. I gifted her an airline ticket to Paris. I knew she wouldn't come back. She assured me of this as she avoided meeting my eye. Her cheeky, licentious looks, which I had liked and gotten used to, were gone. She no longer looked me in the eye, as though she were trying to avoid confronting something that she did not want to see in me. Perhaps she had come to view me as she viewed herself, and her words no longer meant anything. Had I changed that much?

There was nothing to be gained by asking her because she was unwaveringly stubborn. Stubbornness was the weapon with which she had confronted the world, and she made no concessions, not even for me. His entry into our lives had changed the rules of the game, bringing to an end my relationship with her, which I had always described as "strange." She made my dream come true, and I made her wish come true, and that was it.

There was nothing to keep her in the Bataween neighborhood, just as there was nothing to compel her to eat lemons, which she had not tasted since her fetus had been dragged out of her and buried under the lemon tree in the hotel garden. All I could say was that she had brought about my happiness and his. I hoped that the air ticket to Paris brought her happiness.

Father Faridoun gave me absolute happiness, free of all the extra baggage that usually comes with such relationships. He gave strength and clarity of thought. Everything became clearer in his bedroom. Even the noise from the main street outside his window occupied a fond place in my consciousness. I got rid of the boredom that had dominated my life for so long, even before my birth, like a mythical spider that had wrapped me in its sicky secretions from which I thought there could be no salvation. I began to understand the world outside the shadows of the family tree. When he gazed toward me, I would be overcome by a feeling I had not experienced before, and I would merrily wonder how a look could turn into happiness. He wanted to give me a gift that would remain in my memory for ever, hiding deep within the spirit and leaving its mark on the body. His gazes gave me a feeling of pride, as though he were the first person to see me for myself, without my history or my name, or anything else. Just me, Ghosnelban!

He reconciled me with the city in which I was living and whose legacy I carried, although I had not known it outside the map that our families had followed since the times of the Abbasid palaces.

He confessed to me that his fate had brought him out on that foggy October day so that we would meet outside the mansion. He had hesitated before greeting me, and when I had not responded, he attributed that to the conceit of a beautiful girl, or to aristocratic arrogance. He even went further, thinking that it might be because he was of a different religion. His words, uttered in a northern accent that I enjoyed hearing, betrayed a charming shyness. As for me, I was unable to express what I had inwardly experienced that day and in the days following it. I was unable to make sense of the amazing amount of confused and surprising feelings that had overcome me and to put them into words. My tongue was no longer capable of disclosure. How could I describe something that had appeared like a secret gate that is revealed once in a lifetime, fleeting and sharp, transporting us toward eternity?

We understood from the beginning that talking would give rise to questions that would threaten the wounded happiness that we had snatched, so we avoided posing questions or discussing philosophical, religious, and even political issues, for they were swamps that we feared could drown us. We kept questions at bay because we wanted to obscure the clearly obvious fact surrounding us that warned of the impossibility of the survival of such a brilliant relationship at a time like that, and in that city. We impetuously entered a game of self-deception, a deception of time, people, religions, and conventions—in short, a deception of everything. On the white sheets, we were a man and a woman outside boundaries and dimensions. At the beginning, I did not know that our nakedness had different colors. To me, his nakedness was like a cloud that spread drops of rain full of freedom above me, giving me the freedom of roaming an irrational world. To him, my nakedness was dark-colored, frightening him of an obsession of entering deeper into the folds of sin, with all of its joys and high costs. This worried me, but I kept his anxiety at bay, offering him a yearning body that rendered feelings stronger than reason.

I didn't know much about him, but I didn't mind that. I knew full well that outside the confines of that bed, he was a public figure very different from what I knew about him. The occupation and the resulting fanatic instincts that had followed it had forced us all to be secretive with everyone else. The violence that had been unleashed affected everyone, particularly religious minorities, one of which he belonged to.

One day, he seemed sad and preoccupied. He seemed defeated. He had strongly opposed immigration abroad by members of his sect, who had lived in the country since "in the beginning there was the Word." But he was no longer able to stop the rising tide of immigration, and this was putting tremendous pressure on him.

What was occurring in the city troubled both of us. Sometimes we met without thinking of sex. We were searching for an alternative to our human intimacy more than anything else, prompted by a desire to isolate ourselves from the quagmire of violence that had burst the floodgates and was starting to drown everyone, a violence accompanied by unique hysteria. I discovered a human being other than the beautiful lover I had come to know—a sad, perpetually preoccupied, anxious, and wise person, and firm to the point of a cruelty I had not expected of him. One day, he showed me the photograph of a young man in his mid-twenties with a young woman the same age. They were wearing traditional Assyrian clothes, smiling broadly at the camera as though they owned the whole world. He told me they were engineers and had wanted to immigrate to New Zealand after completing all the necessary paperwork at that end. He had convinced them not to immigrate, but they had been killed in a church explosion in Nineveh, their mangled body parts bearing witness to the birth of evil spirits that came from we knew not where! Ever since that incident, he was wracked with a guilt that turned his life into an odious hell. He said he was responsible for their tragic deaths, and that had it not been for him, they would have been happily alive over there in that faraway place. He looked at me, and there was something in his eyes I had never seen before. He then muttered a question that I could not hear clearly. "What do you think of the occupation?"

It was only a question, but it worried me. It was a word

that everyone avoided saying for various reasons, and it became the defining edge between two different worlds that warned of the death ahead: with or against. He thought that because I was of aristocratic descent, I would be "with" because the semi-intellectuals had established this preconceived image of us. I didn't know what he wanted to hear me say. For a moment, I pondered remaining silent to keep questions away from us, but I decided to speak my mind.

"After the occupation, a strange kind of insect that makes an unpleasant sound has taken hold in the garden around our mansion. They're disgusting and black and we have never seen them before. The disturbing noise they make as the night sets in alienates and frightens me."

He stretched out his hand and strongly squeezed mine to convey his strong confusion, as though to alert me to the change that was slowly slouching toward our happiness. A sense of guilt emerged around the sin and love we were indulging in. We made love very seriously, drowning in pleasure and focusing on it details, and we didn't laugh anymore. We tussled with a lightness that was not free of violence and avoided expressions of joy so that we would not provoke sin. I allowed his fleshy lips to devour my body. What lay behind his furrowed brow worried me.

I began to believe that sin was watching us with open eyes until it transformed the happiness we enjoyed into something that only existed in the myths that had left this city with Scheherazade and could not exist at this hate-filled time.

I had not regarded our relationship as a sin, because a sinner must repent, as my sister Rabab had told me after talk spread about my mysterious relationship. "Repent," she said. But for what? The most beautiful times of my life!

When he put his right palm around my neck, curling his four fingers around it and gently stroked my cheek with this thumb as though to reassure himself that I was with him and that I was real and not a phantom, I heard the sound of locks opening in my innermost world, and they continued to perpetually echo in my hearing.

I said to Rabab, "Sinners are the ones who must repent, and I am not a sinner." I was fully convinced that I had not sinned and that Regina had not sinned either.

Our relationship turned into something resembling a thin thread that only I could see, skillfully stretching between sin and repentance. The meeting of pleasure and beauty, only I could see, just like that dawn that my brother Silwan had seen after losing hope that he would live.

Yet in spite of it all, I knew that sin would vanquish me. It had begun to burden him, turning his life into a hell of ceaseless questions of which I was the defining embodiment. He was stalked by a destructive feeling of being torn between the divine mission to which he had consecrated himself and his earthly rights, which I embodied.

Everything in life has a "last time," even life itself. We are mistaken if we do not believe that. The last night with him came. I had not believed that, or perhaps I had not wanted to when I had myself chosen to search for the narrative that had brought me together with him, weaving its threads with my own hands like a priestess consecrated to suffering. I was not like a Jewess awaiting the messiah, nor like the Christian awaiting the Savior, nor like the Muslim awaiting the absent imam. I had taken up my cross myself and had not awaited my salvation. I had chosen my narrative. I began to perceive my body without hostility or fear whenever I passed my hand over its excitable parts, searching out traces of him everywhere, starting with memory and proceeding all the way to the depths of my soul. It was like virgin land that had been sown only once, but its plants lived on forever.

We understood how difficult, even impossible, it was for our love to survive when he himself considered himself as sinful. We fell into a viscous darkness without knowing how to extricate ourselves. With fully open eyes, we consciously accepted a sense of defeat and overwhelming longing for a paganism that disregarded limits and differences—something we had never experienced before.

His beard, which turned gray after the death of the two young people who had dreamed of immigrating to New Zealand, was untrimmed. It seemed as though the atrophy of old age had snuck up on him with amazing speed, like the emaciation that had taken hold of Delilah's body the night she had vanquished Samson, and like the way the black insects with the unpleasant squeak had invaded our garden after the occupation. I was powerless to stop any of it.

CHAPTER 4

DARKNESS

CARAVAGGIO: *THE BEHEADING OF SAINT JOHN THE BAPTIST*

Darkness stalks us, there in the depth of the psyche, biding its time, awaiting the opportunity to transform us into a black nothingness. All the blackness that enveloped our lives was strengthening it.

Mamluka barged into my bedroom with a clear expression of defiance on her face, its hard lines etched onto her features. She had never challenged me before in such a manner, which violated the limits of insolence and threatened a confrontation for which I was completely unprepared and wanted to postpone. I wished I were in a better position, but how? And when?

I imagined defeat, but not then and there. I wanted it while I was standing upright. My god, whenever I tried to compare that creature to the one I had known before the visit of her sister and "his excellency the ambassador and his wife." I would get lost in a vast desert of bewilderment. Nothing remained of the Mamluka I had known. The difference was immense, amazing, reeking of terror. It was as though some evil black power had split her into two unrelated halves.

Despite her almost constant bad temper, she had usually been obedient and had caused no problems, had not been too talkative and had minded her own business. When she had behaved otherwise, we had been grateful because she was acting out of love and was usually right. She had only chatted with my mother, and their years of companionship had transformed their relationship into something akin to friendship.

I knew that my mother had trusted her with many secrets that she had not shared with us, her children, and that this had set her above our other servants. She had served us nimbly, diligently, and with dedication, and had not needed to be told what to do. She had known everything there was to know inside our mansion, but she was so discreet that we had trusted her with our small secrets, and she had never once let us down. She would see and hear but never talk, seeming like a simpleton who knew nothing about life in general or outside her job, which she did to perfection.

Mamluka's movements had been amazingly well-timed. When we needed her, she became all eyes and ears. Otherwise, she had seemed not to be present. She had simply picked up our vibes when we had needed something and had then surprised us. However, it had been so difficult for us to ascertain her needs and wishes, and we had even grown to believe that she had no needs, wishes, or aspirations, that she was simply a robotic human being created to serve others, which meant us!

All that changed dramatically, and she didn't even give me the chance to consider, analyze, or even comprehend it. I was suddenly forced to deal with another person, someone very different from the one I had known, as though I were dealing with her for the first time in my life!

It all happened after her "freedom fighter" nephew and his mother, who was her sister, and his wife visited us. They had barged in on me as though they were violating my stronghold. What did she expect of me? To agree to their request? To not throw them out as calmly as I had done? To thank her and accept the offer of marriage to that "thing" she had brought me? To willingly choose to negate the history of seven generations, as Julnar had done, when she agreed to marry a commoner? Did they believe the slogan on that banner of insanity that was raised in the city after the arrival of the armies of occupation? Did they think that the occupation could erase all differences and barriers and establish new hybrid traditions that would allow them to take over a status that had once been ours?

The day after that shameful visit, she did not come, and that was also a message. I stupidly misinterpreted it because, deep down, I wanted to attribute her absence to being ashamed of her disgustingly slimy behavior and because I wanted to reconfigure things and feelings back to the way they had been. But it seemed she was paving the way for something that had already been arranged, a plan in which she would play the role of mistress of the house after perceiving our weakness in the wake of the transformations that had occurred in the city. Nevertheless, she kept a distance of respect tinged with fear between us.

The seven-day grace period I had been given was all that was left to me in that large mansion, and nothing could halt its passage. Both my sisters had guessed this during our last meeting the previous Thursday. Rabab and Balqis's tears had tasted of a bitter and final farewell. When we embraced, defeat was strongly present. Why was I only able to see that more clearly afterward? What had happened to allow the image of defeat to take shape so clearly?

My front, which has been weak to begin with, crumbled, and my only allies were a brother whose sanity had been stolen on the highway of death and a loyal dog lacking a female. What better opportunity than this to mount a sweeping attack to annihilate the city's history and swallow up the last morsel that had successfully survived the barbarians that had come before?

I began to see Mamluka everywhere, moving heavily with an expression so savage that her eyes could have been whips. I wished she would disappear from my sight, but there she was, making noise deliberately to send me mysterious messages that I couldn't fathom, or waiting for me to break the silence and speak to her frankly. Perhaps she wanted me to hear her give me a choice between accepting her nephew's miserable marriage offer or leaving. But what about Silwan and Guevara?

Rabab and Balqis wanted to leave the country, and Silwan was a heavy burden disrupting their plans. Any suggestion that he should travel or live with them would provoke a storm with their husbands that would have negative consequences. Their message was also clear. Everything seemed as though it had been pre-arranged. I was the only fool left at the mansion.

The noise that Mamluka was deliberately making was destroying my nerves. I could hear her yelling at Guevara, or maybe at Silwan, but the noise was actually directed at me. It wasn't just ordinary noise, but vibes of an evil energy to plant a slow fear within me that would surely spread. I could feel her gazes chasing me everywhere. Her illiteracy was one source of comfort because it limited her ability to chase me. The papers on which I was recording what was happening remained safe from her malevolence, giving me a modicum of freedom in my own mansion.

We all knew that she had a special love for Silwan, and he loved her too, even helping her with her work. Perhaps she saw him as the only surviving male in the family, or as the son she had wished for but never had. She spent a lot of time with him, sitting and looking into his vacantly staring eyes, which resembled black tunnels connected to the hell he had lived through in those desolate regions. She would speak to him, and he remained silent. I had never seen her do that before he had returned from the war. Perhaps she was telling him some of the stories and myths she used to relate to him when he was a child. Silwan would not go to sleep until Mamluka would sit by him and tell him stories that she seemed to invent for him. Perhaps she had cried in front of him that morning, knowing that she, a woman who had been deprived of motherhood, would lose him forever. Was she preparing his obituary as she told him about the plans of her "freedom fighter" nephew, who wanted to take over the mansion, like all the other "freedom fighters" who were biting away at the city? But Silwan was not dead yet!

Was she planning his death, to kill him, to kill us if I thought of resisting the black plague sweeping through the city? Had they not sent me a bullet in an envelope? Had her nephew sent that bullet to scare me and force me to marry him and accompany him to Athens to confer a borrowed grandeur on his low status?

Like a bolt of lightning from the unknown, like the black thoughts that come from a time and place we do not know, I remembered an event from long ago during the last stages of my father's illness with terminal cancer. I had forgotten it, or perhaps I convinced myself that I had. That day, Rabab's husband, Raouf, had brought some cyanide from his pharmacy on the insistence of my father, who had wanted to end his unbearable pain. We had realized that day that my father was contemplating suicide, but as usual we had remained silent. Ever since Julnar's departure, silence had been all we had known. We had clung to it like a powerful god, not exchanging a single word about her disappearance with one another, for we were both the masters and slaves of silence, excelling at playing its game and calibrating our rhythm to its eternal rhythm. The trace of secretly shed tears that we quickly wiped away for fear they would be seen were all that could be detected. Rabab had sat in the reception room, her flushed face betraying her struggle with words and tears and foreshadowing the future confronting us. We were not in the habit of posing urgent questions. What was the use? He had decided, and it was necessary for all of us to help him—through a conspiracy of silence—to end his pain.

When he died, no one asked my mother the question that was on everyone else's mind. My mother was the family's keeper of secrets, a role that women traditionally play. Had my father died of natural causes, or had he ingested the poison that Raouf had brought? Silence stretches a curtain of comfortable mystery and it therefore saved us from the confusion that affected us all. We adeptly maneuvered around the question because we had not wanted to bring up the issue to protect our fake sense of security. His sudden death had been a "mercy," because it had freed him from his pains and spared the rest of us the futility of asking about the fate of the small blue bottle that Raouf had brought from his pharmacy. But the question came crashing back into my consciousness after all those years. Where was that blue bottle that had held within its dark insides, shielded from light by navy blue, an elixir capable of snuffing out life and whipping it away forever? An answer of yes or no could have awakened all the monsters crouching in the dark corners of our family's history.

I had not thought about this before, nor had it occurred to me in my worst nightmares to ask my mother, who would have definitely said she knew nothing about it, pursing her lips in a manner that I knew well—the most eloquent response to a question I should have never asked.

Mamluka definitely knew the fate of that dark bottle that carried cold death within it. Had the time come to ask the question?

I mulled over that painful subject as my gaze scanned the seven paintings and stopped at a painting I knew well. I adored the lines and colors in each of that artist's paintings, which numbered over seventy. Caravaggio, that equivocating Italian magician, who had inhabited that ambiguous space between fact and myth. During his short life, he had burst into the world of painting like a fierce storm and was considered the spiritual father of modern art. The king of light and darkness, the absurd murderer, the narcissist who had enjoyed megalomania, which he had immortalized in several paintings. The wanted criminal in medieval times who spent his time roaming cities and states as he escaped until he found the ultimate solution in death and decided to return to Rome to savor his death. He decided to enter the heart of the story to become the story...darkness and light!

Caravaggio's painting *The Beheading of Saint John the Baptist* depicts that the love that afflicted the mind of the beautiful dancer Salome for John the Baptist, sparking her desire for blatant revenge. She was high born, and the most powerful people would bow at her feet, yet the mystic John, who was in search of truth, had spurned her love and desire. She had begged him, but he had continued to reject her, prompting her in the end to have his head cut off and placed on a golden platter that she held as she danced in front of others.

It was a precious painting in which Caravaggio had been able to capture and immortalize the moment of terror, outdoing hundreds of artists who had dealt with that exciting subject over the centuries.

I recalled that my mother had once asked my grandfather why he had chosen that painting, which she disliked because of the violence it evoked, betraying her secret wish that it should be removed from the wall of the large reception room.

My grandfather looked at her with a sarcastic smile on his lips, which were topped by a well-groomed, thick white moustache. Perhaps that look was enough to convey the message that "When I am dead, you can do as you like." But he backed down, out of respect to the woman who served the family with such dedication, and his expression changed to one of tolerance as he abandoned that hostile response. Speaking to her with his usual extreme politeness, he explained that the painting's artistic value far exceeded the importance of the blood depicted in it.

Had I been answering her question, I would have explained that artistic value to my dear mother by saying, "The aesthetics of that brilliant painting do not only focus on violence, as the depiction of John the Baptist's slaughter would first suggest. The beauty resides in following the fragmented terror on the faces in the painting, including Salome's beautiful face, as the ugly beheading takes place. Fear and the shadow of sin that dominates everyone takes them to the point of no return, shaking the biblical narrative that solely accuses Salome of murder.

Caravaggio focuses on the insistence of the father, whose face appears ready to carry out the mission as though it were an unstoppable fate, an insistence that exceeds his daughter's keenness for the completion of the beheading, whereas Salome simply carries the golden platter she will hold up with the saint's severed head as she dances. The beat of the drum to which she will perform her dance will continue to be transmit-ted along the suffocating waves of memory, generation after generation, making it history's most famous dance. The face of the dancer betrays no trace of happiness. She almost seems like nothing more than an obedient young girl preparing to play a predetermined role, a fate that resembles a light falling from the sky on the scene of the crime amid the darkness surrounding everyone, depicted by Caravaggio with extreme skill. See, dear mother, there are only two witnesses watching from behind the iron bars of the big window overlooking the scene—seized by amazement, curiosity and dread in equal measure—as though attempting to convey the tale to future generations so that no one will forget John the Baptist and Salome."

For a moment, I could no longer see the face of the slain man in the painting. Instead, I saw the face of my brother, Silwan. The two faces merged and melded into each other: the two bodies, the two fates. A soft black power seduced me into closing my eyes as I trembled with the impact of the approaching idea. I immediately realized that that power would take me mercilessly along a course that had been drawn since eternity, and I could only obey as a human obsessed with the idea of murder.

I trembled and then jumped up, not knowing where to go, a black suffocating smoke rising from deep within me, blinding me and tempting me to murder, telling me that it would provide salvation. Yes, Silwan's death would allow the family's journey to reach its fateful end. It was as though my body had been affected by a strong electric current. I turned my face away from the instigating painting, then slowly gave in to a strange desire to look at it again. Yes, they resembled each other. Actually, they were the same person. I was attracted to the idea that all solutions lay in Silwan's death. He must die! I must liberate him from the constant nightmare that was slowly and mercilessly savaging his spirit. I decided that my hand must not shake as I brought him out forever from that gray area called the land of insanity between life and death. I would complete the task that fate had not finished.

I drew closer to the painting to ascertain whether the face belonged to the slain man or to Silwan. I wasn't able to distinguish them anymore. I saw Caravaggio's signature. It was the only one of his paintings that he had signed. Why had he chosen this particular painting to break his habit? And why had he chosen to put his name within the spot of dark red blood flowing from the victim's neck? Questions that would continue to generate theories, none of which would be solid enough to bring Caravaggio out of the deep darkness he inhabited or dispel his great ambiguity. But they inspired me with the idea of killing Silwan, whose death would provide final deliverance of a burden we could no longer carry.

I didn't notice her coming into the room. Had she knocked, or had she just barged in with an innate barbarism that years of cultivation had not succeeded in eradicating? Whatever the case may have been, Mamluka stood in the middle of the room, seeming to me like the messenger of death. She seemed impatient, as though preparing to say something rude, the effects of which I sensed before she uttered it. But she stopped when she saw the fiery look in my eyes that she knew well. In a commanding tone which she had no choice but to obey and which reminded her that I was still the one giving orders in the mansion, even if only temporarily, I asked her about the dark-colored bottle. She hesitated momentarily, as though she were confused and defeated. Nevertheless, she did not lower her gaze, throwing me a defiant look, then turning on her heel and leaving the room without saying a word. She didn't need to ask me why I was asking about that bottle. She knew me well enough to understand my thinking. I thought she was the only one who had known the secret of my relationship with Father Faridoun. Although we had not talked about it, because our conventions made it impossible for us to have such private chats with the servants, there were many signals that made me certain that she knew.

I tried to remain in the sitting room all day to keep away from Silwan and Guevara. I didn't want to see them, perhaps because I feared weakness or hesitation. The sitting room's walls were covered with memories that breathed. It was the last refuge where I could shelter away from the weakness I wrestled with as it tried to defeat me. Outside the sitting room door, everything was working against me: the city, its inhabitants, the occupation, even the weather and the dust in which we were drowning since the defeat at Hafr al-Batin, feelings loaded with lots of negative energy against everything: hatred, counterfeit, lies, bad language, dirty clothes, barbaric noise, the whips of a debauched sun, ugliness, bad odors, unrestrained killing and poisonous tongues inciting sectarianism and turning religion into an instrument to deepen that rabid, destructive conflict. Where could I turn to escape the hell that conjured up another of the paintings hanging in the reception room? The painting of the obsessed Dutch painter Hieronymus Bosch. Was it death?

"From dust to dust" is a biblical expression that epitomizes all life and which Father Faridoun often quoted. Strange how I never dared to mention his name without prefacing it with

"Father" or "Reverend." In bed, he would become "him," but outside it he would immediately become "Father Faridoun."

Dust was submerging the city and everyone in it, trying to reclaim it from humankind. In my childhood, I believed it to be an eternal city. How naïve that belief now seemed. I had not known that dust was nature's eternal secret weapon against us. Dust was being piled onto us just as it would be over a dead body in the grave. But what would be the fate of the city's glory, embellished with epics and myths, with the men and women who had lived and died in it, its writers, poets, philosophers, Sufis, rulers, builders of its glory, its concubines and servants, its kings and tramps, its noblemen and rabble. Could all that turn into a faint myth like Babel, Tibah, and Samarkand? Could Baghdad become one of those once-dominant cities that were destroyed?

Why me, who hated everything in it, and loved everything in it? Love and hate were part of a vicious circle that I could find no way out of.

The day after the letter containing the threat arrived, the dust was at its worst. I usually hated the dust and considered it a bad omen. It gave me a unique kind of headache tinged with depression, suggesting thoughts of suicide, causing me breathing difficulties, and putting me in a bad mood. But on that day, I was strangely comfortable with it. I might not have been exaggerating when I wrote that I needed it. I sat in the sitting room watching its fine particles swimming in the air, enabling me to forge harmony with my new ideas and to surround them with evil intentions that began to take a clear shape. The dust enveloped the idea of murder with a deceptive and confusing coating, blunting its moral sharpness. It was the dust from which we came and to which we would return.

From my spot where I breathed in the dust and communicated with it, through the large window overlooking the veranda, I caught sight of Silwan striding into the depths of the large garden that was immersed in dust. Guevara was following him and he seemed different. He was no longer just a dog, but a hunchbacked elder immersed in deep thought, his slow and burdened steps making it seem as though he was walking toward death more purposefully than Silwan.

For a moment, I got a fleeting suspicion that someone was calling to them from within the dust that was coming down from the sky as they walked like two beings seized by the strength of that call. From above, we all seemed like complicated lines on a fortune-teller's sand slate.

Visibility was limited to one meter, beyond which the scene thickened into a ruinous vacuum with an appetite for swallowing all creatures. Where were they going?

I wanted to get up and call them, but something caught hold of my light blue dress, which Balqis had brought me from Madrid for my last celebrated birthday. I put my hand over my mouth to stifle a scream. All pleasures had been superseded by an eternity reminiscent of oblivion and seemed very far away and even unreal, even though they could be remembered.

What was preventing me from calling Silwan, who had been swallowed up by the ruinous vacuum? Was it the dust, or had I perhaps entered into a hallucinatory phase and begun listening to a voice from deep within saying, "He's going to his long-overdue death. Let him be!"

Sitting on the expensive green leather chair that my grandfather had bought from Istanbul, I stretched my upper body around, trying to open my eyes as wide as possible so that my sight would penetrate deep into the dust, to see the terrifying ruinous vacuum and its dark insides as it swallowed them up.

I wept bitterly, longing to throw myself to the wolf that was inexorably approaching. I had needed that crying fit. I had never done it before. I had not cried at the death of my father, or of my mother, or at the city's occupation. I had simply been seized by a great and inexplicable anger. Their deaths and the city's occupation were similar—the outcome of betrayal, which I cannot stand. My tears had flowed profusely when my grandfather had left me and decided to join the kingdom of death, as in Arnold Böcklin's painting. I had been very attached to him, to his shadow, the well-arranged words he used to utter with elegant deliberation, his charming aristocratic moves that no one could match, his rare facial expressions that carefully constituted the most appropriate impression of any situation he was facing, his love of the arts, and his impeccable taste.

The dust began to infiltrate the mansion like an inevitable death, like a curse reminiscent of nothingness. It piled up in layers, even though the doors and windows had been tightly shut. It piled up challengingly before our eyes, reminding us of our total inability to stop or limit it, as though it wanted to emphatically remind us of the inevitable message of destruction epitomized by "from dust to dust."

I had fallen in love with Father Faridoun in a single moment because he resembled my grandfather. At first, I had not realized that I was searching for surviving traces of my grandfather until I had seen Father Faridoun's smile and realized how similar it was to the Pasha's. Father Faridoun's unique smile was like a joyous ray of sun on a cold winter's day. Even in the scent of his body—I was searching for a scent that was long gone.

I loathe weeping. I abhor the cheapness and submission that go with it, just as I detest weakness, impotence, and humiliation. In spite of that, I cried over Silwan's fate, which seemed to have been decided the day we received that barbaric bullet, which was lying in a miserable envelope in one of the desk drawers. A declaration of utter impotence, like paralysis. Was all that feeling churning around within my tumultuous psyche, or was it part of that sad dark thread wrapped around the occupied city that the dust was preparing to finally envelope?

I lost track of the time I spent staring in terror and submission at the deep layers of dust that were getting thicker and more savage. I no longer experienced the darkness that occupied visible areas because the color of the dust transformed everything into a uniform state of ruin, and it was difficult to distinguish the calamities within it. Dust has the ability to uproot color and glorify khaki depression. Khaki was the color that had been spread since the first coup, and all subsequent coups stuck to it. Even the occupation, which came on the pretext of liberating us, was khaki. And when the khaki dissolved, it was replaced by an even more abominable color: blackness descended.

Where had those beautiful, elegant colors that were still stuck in my memory since the mansion garden party gone?

I sensed her hissing breath behind me, just like the snake that had wrapped itself around the tree of knowledge and seduced the first human into sinfulness. Mamluka was behind me, and I didn't need to turn around to verify this. She was there, her hateful presence bordering on a sense of malicious joy that I feared. For the first time, I was scared of being alone with her. How strangely feelings had changed.

I only needed to turn halfway to see her familiar hand with the faded tattoo that indicated her origins as she placed the dark blue bottle on the small table beside me. It contained sudden death that comes from the dark places that Caravaggio had excelled at depicting in all his paintings, a darkness that leaves behind a lasting scent that transcends time and seduces one to drift into it, merging with it and disappearing into its amorphous gloom. Lights coming from unknown places are usually heavenly and inaccessible to the weak. But darkness seems more aggressive and poised to pounce, emerging from Caravaggio's paintings to envelope everything. The ugliest darkness lurks in the depths, our depths.

I assumed that the bottle was empty, or so I hoped. But when I picked it up with my fingertips, my hand shook uncontrollably, and I realized that it was full of death.

She did not need to speak. We were still able to communicate with the least number of words, despite the grayness of the chasm that was widening between us. When I had asked her that morning what had happened to the bottle, she immediately knew which bottle I was asking about and what I was thinking.

Soon, it would be dinner time, and the bottle's contents

would be part of one or more dishes, it made no difference. I would not ask, and she did not expect me to.

My hand continued to shake after she took the bottle away. The human frailty that I detested and considered to be only fit for the weak was controlling me and exposing me before my servant.

The idea of Silwan's death raced through my blood like a pack of hungry wolves. Would I be able to tame or control them, or at least rein in their recklessness? The idea was smoothly taking shape in my mind's eye, within the corners of my mind and on my tongue. Although one part of me rejected it, it had become stronger than me.

Good and evil are two sides of the same coin. All you need to do is to turn it over onto one side or the other and you fall under the spell of the side facing you. My acquiescence to ending Silwan's life was not an absolute evil. What was the point of living in the shadow of helplessness? His helplessness to free himself from the claws of the insanity that had taken hold of him, his inability to survive in a city full of evil people.

Dignity, the only value that stands above good and evil and imbues them with meaning, was on its way to extinction. It was better for an individual to die with dignity than to live without it. That was not just empty talk. Weakness and humiliation were harder than death. His death would allow me to save his dignity, which would otherwise be trampled, since I was no longer able to protect him. They were stealing everything, even people's dignity.

The occupation had awakened the spirit of absolute evil within us, unleashing all our latent violence and turning it in on us. It transformed us into animals fighting over a dead body. How could I possibly defend him amidst human groups that did not even comprehend their own evil and blindness?

I certainly still loved Silwan, but what meaning did love have at such a time in a city whose inhabitants were vying to cannibalize its best people, reveling in chaos and boasting of treason and depravity?

A clear and comfortable feeling came over me. Silwan must depart life with dignity.

In the evening, Silwan's voice filled the mansion as though he had just been born. I had no idea when the dust had pushed him out of its depths again, although I had been expecting that and watching out for it for hours. He walked in with an inexplicable mirth in his eyes and addressed me with an affection that I had not seen him display since his return from the desert death trap sprung for him by the cowboys.

He walked into the sitting room and asked, "Will you be sitting here for long?" Pointing to the dog, he said, "Come on, we're starving."

I almost broke down in tears and nearly scuppered my plans, which Mamluka had set up with her usual perfection. She looked at me, awaiting a word to change the plan and serve the food without the lethal poison. She loved Silwan as much as I did, and maybe more. By striking an implicit deal with her, I was not granting her salvation. Rather, I had a devilish desire to avenge myself on her by killing my brother.

I pretended to be busy gathering up my papers and smoothing out my blue dress, so that they would not notice my confusion or the evil expression on my face, although I was not sure that my feet would allow me to get up. I was scared that my legs would give way and that I would collapse in tears at the feet of Mamluka, the mansion's new mistress.

His death, our death, was a thunderous, driverless train that would ultimately pluck us up from our stations one after the other. I could almost hear its deafening sound. I finally got up and walked toward him, trying as much as possible not to look back, although I could hear her hissing, mixed with a sad moan. I stood before him, looking into his confused eyes, and she continued to await the answer to his question. My God, the sudden puzzling confusion in his eyes could have turned into a sharp blade that he could slaughter me with. I embraced him and kissed him between the eyes in the hope of extinguishing the flame of his beautiful peaceful expression that foretold dark endings. We both blushed, because I had not done so before, or since his return from "there." I was willing to do more than that, to hold him close, weep with him, in the hope of wiping away that calm expression that was stabbing me, and I felt my knees going loose.

I wanted her to see the tragedy in our eyes, to feel the approaching transgression Mamluka had caused, the fear that had expanded within me. I wanted her to see something that would remind her of the approaching death, not of the past. She and I could hear death's footsteps as it walked with unbridled savagery through the mansion, which had begun to sink into Caravaggio's darkness.

I slipped my hand beneath his arm and asked him to lead me to the dinner table. Guevara followed us. He seemed hesitant, as though he were listening to the sound of death's footsteps, which his sensitives ears did not miss. Silwan was the only innocent, entering Caravaggio's painting without knowing what role he would be playing. We knew he would play the hero's role: the slaughtered John the Baptist, for whose blood Mamluka would seal the end of our era and the beginning of another. The odor of fresh blood permeated the mansion and would never leave it. A new soul would join those that had disappeared but not departed.

Silwan led me to the table like a handsome aristocratic gentleman. I longingly thought of the beauty of a bygone time, and it banished all the feelings of weakness that had assailed me. Mamluka stood at the edge of Caravaggio's painting waiting to witness the moment of John the Baptist's death. Deep within her rang the bells of the savage joy that had once rung deep within Ibn al-Alqami, glorifying all betrayals and declaring him their master. Treachery had always been noisy.

There she was, ridding herself of the story of her life, which she had betrayed: Silwan. The tale was tinged with equal amounts of love and hate. She was drawing close to the end that she had planned, so that absolute darkness would prevail forever.

I took my seat at the head of the table, playing my role for the last time as the heiress of the glory that had begun to audibly fracture as the Western tanks had rolled down the asphalt of the alleys of the city that my ancestors had built, and on whose ancient walls al-Hallaj had been crucified.

My brother sat to my right and Guevara settled on the Italian tiles, closing his eyes with a strange submission that reminded me of a picture of his namesake, the handsome revolutionary, who lay dead in the jungle with his eyes closed, surrounded by the smiling men who had hunted him down.

The flowers I had cut that morning were at the center of the table, but they looked wilted. The empty plates sat before us, surrounded by forks, knives, and spoons. On my signal, which she had awaited, Mamluka came forward and filled the plates with vegetable soup. Its deceptively appetizing aroma floated across the table.

Silwan sipped his first spoonful, then looked at Mamluka to express his appreciation as he had learned to do in his youth. She was unable to meet that look with the gratitude she was accustomed to showing or to stay on to wish him "*bon appétit*."

She quietly withdrew to the kitchen, leaving us to our confusing deaths. I picked up my first spoonful of soup, not knowing whether my plate contained any of the poison that my father had taken one day long ago. But I was seized by a powerful feeling of defiance that stopped me from focusing on that lethal question. What joy could life hold among humans with polluted minds such as the city's inhabitants?

I did not want to stop consuming more soup until I had completely finished as Silwan had already done.

As soon as we put our empty plates aside, she served the main courses. I paid no attention to them at first because I was exploring the corners of my mouth with my tongue to investigate a strange taste that seemed to have settled in some of them. For a moment, it seemed that something tasted strange, but I wasn't sure. Perhaps it was a new kind of spice mix. Mamluka was well-versed in the secrets of spices, unlike me. I had been uninterested in the art of cooking and had never considered it to be one of my priorities. I had insisted on avoiding it, despite my mother's continuous urgings. After our cook, Mary, had traveled to the north to await death in the sunny plains, Mamluka had taken over that task, and had proven herself to be a good cook.

Once I had finished exploring my mouth for strange tastes, I began to carefully listen to the vibrations of my intestines just in case I could detect pain coming on gradually, colic, nausea, or anything indicating that the end was coming. But none of that happened, and it seemed that only my mind was affected. I almost chuckled with panic.

The main course consisted of a roast with vegetables. In bygone days, my father had usually carved and served the meat. After his death, Silwan had taken that task upon himself, and we had entrusted it to him to show our pride in his role as the man of the family. But after his return from the land of death, he had refused to perform it with a strange insistence. That evening, I had wanted to watch him doing it again, perhaps for the last time. I was like someone who had been sentenced to death doing something for the last time. I gently asked him if he would do it. At first, he seemed confused and hesitant. But he looked into the eyes of Guevara, who was closer to him than I or any other creature was, and he seemed to draw courage from him. He carved the roast, although he seemed to have lost his former dexterity. That pleased me, and for a brief moment, I thought of pulling out of the hellish plan that we seemed to be following as though we were hypnotized or under a spell. I looked at Mamluka, who had covered her mouth with her hand to stop herself from gasping. She too had forgotten her role for a brief moment and was treating all of us for the last time as though we still belonged to one another as we had in times gone by.

He filled my plate with meat and vegetables, and then his. We ate our food with an accursedly good appetite, and I wished for death. Death's angel, Mamluka put down a plate in front of Guevara. It contained some bones, which he liked, and I could hear them cracking between his teeth as he enjoyed his meal. Silwan and I did not converse. He merely remarked on the tastiness of the food, which Mamluka had made an effort to prepare well. I then drank some Arabic coffee, but he preferred to have some fruit. I wanted to be done with that funeral-like dinner, which dragged on as my imagination toyed with a wish as vague as a mirage that it was all a nightmare made of the same dust that had swallowed up the city after the occupation, and that it would soon end.

I wished everyone a goodnight and went upstairs to my room, clinging to the shadows of the dusty wish and the thought that tomorrow would bring us real hope in life. One day, Father Faridoun had kissed my forehead and whispered movingly, "The age of miracles is not over."

I lay down on my bed fully clothed, having decided to sleep in my day clothes for fear that others would see me in my underwear after my death. But I couldn't shut my eyes because suspense and anxiety banished drowsiness. I jumped out of bed in panic. I realized that Mamluka had not poisoned me. She had only poisoned Silwan. But how could she have done that when we were both eating the same food? She must have slipped it in with the fruit, which I did not eat. She knew

I didn't like to eat fruit after dinner. But why did she not want to include me in her feelings of hatred? I couldn't understand where those feeling had come from.

I remained in that state for several hours, listening for the signs of death. My senses were in a state of heightened alert. I could hear strange noises coming from the floor below. I went to the door of my room and put my ear to it to try to make out the commotion, which was like death's footsteps. The commotion grew louder, impervious to my terror, and it was mixed in with muttering and human or demonic voices, although I could not distinguish one from the other. All I could feel was terror, which began to wrap itself around me like clinging bindweed. The one thing I still trusted was that Mamluka would be able to handle everything without kicking up a fuss or making a mistake. I plucked up enough courage to slightly open the door to find an explanation for those muffled voices that were rising from the bottom of hell, but I didn't succeed. Mystery had surrounded everything in the mansion since we had received the threatening bullet.

I shut the door and returned to my bed. I closed my eyes and tried to sleep.

I wanted to sleep to avoid witnessing the outcome of the crime I had committed or any knowledge of its details as Mamluka dealt with it with her typical attention to detail. The only image that remained with me as I drifted off to sleep was of the faces of those who had come to ask for my hand. It was typical of the city that there was no shouting when crimes were committed at night, and the city would overlook the biggest ones.

The last image in my overburdened imagination was that of the two witnesses watching the slaughter of John the Baptist through a window in Caravaggio's painting. Would sorrow protect us from guilt?

I thought of the fate of Guevara, and I was surprised that he was making no sounds. Why, when he was so hostile to strangers, was he silent despite all the commotion in that netherworld that Mamluka was mistress of?

Chapter Five

DEFEAT

Diego Velázquez: Mars Resting

I woke from being half asleep but did not open my eyes. I kept them closed for fear of seeing a new reality that I did not want to see. I wanted to block my ears so that I would not hear the loud, hissing voice of tragedy. I tried to quickly recall where I was and where I had been. Had I really fallen asleep?

Until that morning, I had never known that nightmares live in a gray area between wakefulness and sleep, like a bed of painful thorns that I was forced to wade through, certain that they had nailed me excruciatingly to their cross. It was a thorny area full of devilishly piercing questions.

The gates of the tragic world I had entered had closed behind me on the first day of the end of one era and the beginning of another, with the arrival of a bullet that rudely announced the era of the rabble. Another thing I had lost for good was proper sleep. But how could I tackle the series of defeats that were like a violent torrent, uprooting all the principles I had believed in?

I quickly surveyed the room, the ceiling, the walls, the door, and all the things familiar to me as I searched for a lost feeling that would give me at least a bit of security. Everything was in its place. "Life without values is like living in a rubbish dump." I don't know why I recalled that resounding comment that my father used to utter whenever he was dismayed by the cheapness that was submerging our lives. I closed my eyes as I resisted a barely conscious wish to voluntarily descend to the bottom, the bottom of the filth that we had always avoided and held ourselves above. I had a desire to try it, to wallow in it, to squeeze the word "filth" to the very last drop and drink it. I was no longer able to ignore it, or remain above it. Filth entailed benefits that tempted everyone to be folded into it with a hysterical, heathen, ritualistic joy—our golden calf. Filth had been with us for a long time, and in my naivete I had deluded myself that I was able to remain above it. I had never imagined that my obsession with avoiding it would lend it a stubbornness and an insistence on spreading. Filth does not wait for someone to choose to descend into it. It has a phenomenal ability to climb quickly, expanding among us the city's thorny riverbanks that have surrendered to filth.

The light seeping through the openings in the curtain indicated that morning had arrived. But it wasn't a morning befitting Baghdad's sun, well-known for its boldly brilliant light, a sun that drove shadows into oblivion as it proudly shone from its zenith, turning us into shadowless creatures.

The sun sent forth dull, weak, soulless rays that almost seemed incapable of providing light. Its sad light resembled the city's fate, which was leading it toward massacres. The sun was refusing to play its eternal role. Its light was dim and seemed defeated as it wrestled with nihilistic dust in a battle that had already been decided in favor of its enemy. It was a light befitting the mysterious fate that had befallen Silwan and Guevara.

I recalled details of the Velázquez painting hanging on the wall of the large sitting room in which he depicted the brave god of war, the good-looking young Mars, not the way other painters usually did, but as a weak, tired old man who had fought the last of his mythical battles and had collapsed as he begged death to save him.

I was once more seized by a hysterical anxiety. I gazed all around me, looking for something unknown. I was trying to escape thinking of the previous night's events and wanted to make sure I was still alive, even though the word "life" seemed incompatible with that light, which conjured up the shadows of the dead, the departed, and the murdered.

I moved my tongue over my rigid, salty lips, which had borne an expression of haughty seriousness all my life, a frown that I had inherited like an Abbasid curse through seven previous generations. Father Faridoun's lips had been like the forbidden fruit that I had taken pleasure in without heed to any warnings.

My lips were like a drought-stricken land that had not received any water since the walls of Baghdad had fallen beneath the hooves of the occupiers as they entered beneath the cloaks of the modern descendants of Alqam, who had let the Tartars into the city.

I rolled my tongue towards my throat, which was even drier, disgusted with my ability to accumulate so much salt on my lips.

I tried closing my eyes again, but I was terrified of returning to that thorny patch full of prickly, diabolical questions.

The mysterious muttering voices that had kept me awake the day before sounded more impertinent and oblivious to my presence. They prompted me to use my last remaining strength to raise myself and sit on the edge of the bed. I was the last in a dynasty that was going extinct.

The voices alerted me that I was on the brink of a major transformation, an era of nihilistic chaos that wanted to swallow me up and remove me. I listened to the gibberish uttered by the voices below, searching for her voice, which rose above the other serpent-like noises every now and then, eventually turning into something akin to a siren announcing the imminent catastrophe. It was a voice that carved unknown, indelible tracks into the soul. I knew her voice well. It had recently taken on a renegade tone like those of rusting iron teeth. I listened more carefully to pick up what was being said, but there were too many voices, and I didn't succeed.

I suddenly realized that they were on the second floor. The hissing was getting closer. Their voices were a warning of spreading evil. I jumped up as though I had been stung, not knowing how I could confront the cataclysmic challenge that was crawling toward my last remaining bastion. As I faced up to the challenge, my limbs no longer conspired against me. I stared at my bed, which I had just left, with wide open eyes, wondering with a stupidity that confused me, whether I was the one who had actually slept in it.

The dust was still seeping in and piling up in layers with a disgusting malevolence. My watch indicated it was ten o'clock.

I instinctively turned toward the large mirror hanging on the wall and I almost screamed, but my strangulated vocal cords let me down and prevented me from wailing. The pungent salt piled on my lips seeped into my soul and destroyed any perceptible light. To whom did that face hanging on the surface of the mirror belong?

Had it not been for the blue dress from Madrid that I had been wearing from the day before, I would not have recognized myself. I gently passed my hand over it to make sure I was wearing it and that I was myself. I experienced its former beauty. I only chose to wear a few of the clothes hanging in my wardrobe. The rest were like a numerical memory that referred to the occasions and dates on which I had bought or warn them, awaiting their turn for me to wear them one day that might never arrive so that they could reactivate their secret relationship with my body. But to whom did that face belong? To my grandmother? To my mother? Maybe to one of my sisters, or perhaps to all the family's females, and even its males? Seven documented generations. The only face that refused to appear was that of Julnar. That rebellious and perpetually rejectionist face, dreaming of individualism, determined to cling to its own ego, which was out of harmony with the rest of us. She was the only one who had discovered the secret early and so had decided to escape from this crude game of reincarnation. I had heard that she had a daughter, and I strongly hoped that she did not share our pampered and privileged looks, and that she would always live outside the Abbasid circle.

I went toward the door, although I had no real wish to leave the room, because staying in it kept my fears at bay, comfortably isolated from the torture of confronting the frightening hatred that had started moving to swallow us up. But my fear that one of them would burst into my room was greater, prompting me to go out and confront the danger outside rather than in my room.

I slowly drew near to the balustrade and caught sight of them. Many strangers were cheekily moving about in the mansion's main hallway. They spoke in loud voices and exchanged vulgar laughs that exploded within my kingdom like smart precision bombs damaging the depths of my soul. A woman stopped in the middle of the hallway and looked straight up at me. It was the same woman with the insolent expression who had come to ask for my hand for her "resistance fighter" husband. Obscenity personified. No, even more than that, her gloating overflowed with a torrent of hostile feelings that surprised me, and her clear destructive ability scared me.

I took two steps back to avoid her gaze, which I could stand no longer. I tried to avoid her hissing smile, to avoid all of them, to block out their voices. I quickly headed upward toward the mansion's roof, where I would be alone under the sky. They would be out of my sight, and their words, which were like fragmented nails, would no longer be audible. I wanted to get away from them at whatever cost, to simply make them disappear with a haughtiness that I had inherited, to confront them with the weapon of contempt. I had no other weapons.

I opened the door and was assailed by the same dull light, swimming in cold dust particles. I curled up near the door and threw up everything—that last supper and them. The vomit had a yellow color and white bubbles, which exploded, and the mixture simply merged with the color of dirt.

I felt relief, like someone who had thrown off a heavy burden. Mamluka's siren-like voice did not reach that spot. I had exited the circle of evil that had been set up by the gaze of the cheeky fat woman. The faint sick sunlight suddenly took on a sense of comfort. It was no longer capable of lighting up the city or resisting the dust that was descending all over the place. The dust thickened, as though to remind me of oblivion. I drew close to the fence surrounding the roof. It was made of black iron and included carvings of mythical plants. Its design resembled the walls of Parisian verandas. There were a few neglected items about that I had not seen before. I had not been on the roof for many years, perhaps not since I was a child. My god, how time had passed.

From such a height, the city appeared strange to me. It was like a table with the remains of rotting food on it, and the people were like insects jostling one another within its insides. I was taken aback by the amount of ruin that had befallen it. Ruin was piling over it, one era after the next, just as the dust was piling over it day after day. The feeling of wanting to vomit persisted, although my insides were empty of everything, except the remains of the aged city's appearance. Was this really the city that I had been refusing to leave? Was it possible for me not to have sensed all that destruction before and to have only discovered it as I was preparing to cast a farewell look over it? It was a city preparing to hide among stacks of books, after all the statues and monuments that told its tale had been looted or blown up.

I drew closer to the iron fence to look at the street outside the mansion's gate. People scurried about like ants. Their movements seemed meaningless and aimless, complete chaos. I could almost sense their dismal feelings like disgusting waste, savage feelings all over the place. Their behavior conjured up a memory of the wild animals in Silwan's hallucinations. Had Silwan been hallucinating, or had he been expressing his perspective on those whose feelings had died?

Looking at them from above as the dust descended on them and obscured their features, they seemed shadowy and unreal, but I knew that they had a dense, albeit meaningless presence that filled the streets, alleyways, and the horizon. Even behind their half-open doors and closed windows, their feelings seeped out like waste to an unknown destination. Crowds, crowds, crowds competing with zero in its nihilism, but what about me?

From such a comfortable height, Baghdad seemed like a mythical city that had borne the brunt of the Lord's ire, entering into the holy books as an archetypal ruined city, in which some of our ruins had been etched. That day, the city seemed like a feast that dogs were biting at, and death was humiliating in the hope that it would wake up to what was happening to it. But our tears were hidden like tears.

I fervently wished that I could cover my skin with a veil that would protect me from the flood of tawdriness. Writing was my last protective layer that gave me the ability to confront, and words were the pegs upon which I hung the image of history, giving me a comfortable dose of missing humanity in this repulsive city. Our family had taken refuge in words for a long time, in their magic, their puzzles, their successive layers, their amazing eloquence, and their deep secrets that they only impart to those who love them. We would transcend the first trivial level and leave it to others, immersing ourselves in the beauty of their eloquence, which sprang from a deep-seated memory of the city we had built out of poetry, art, and beauty, keeping track of its transformations, consciousness, and unique Sufism.

From that comfortable height, I cast a final look over the dying city I could barely recognize. It had expanded a lot and been invaded by ignorance, poverty, and bad taste—architectural sins that had nothing to do with us. I was scared of those neighborhoods that were being built and were expanding and multiplying like some contagious disease. We never went near them, remaining content with our old, neglected neighborhoods through which an Abbasid sap had run, and I would leave the echo of my footsteps there as my ancestors had done.

Ugliness no longer attracted attention because its opposite, which emphasized its ugliness, no longer existed. The people running around me did not think of beauty, so they were not bothered by the ugliness around them. It had swallowed up everyone, until we too had become enveloped by it.

I felt that our city was searching for its fault line, which would lead it to its sad end. I felt a loss that strengthened my resignation. No one feared for its sad collapse, its defeat before the invaders and traitors, a defeat like that of Mars, the handsome God of war, who had aged in the Velázquez painting hanging in the sitting room.

There was still some defiance deep within me. Perhaps it was the last of my determination. I was the descendent of the first builders of this city, which was constructed of words before stones. It seemed to me to have grown old, like Mars, but I still carried its glory, which would persist even as something past.

I went downstairs with an overwhelming determination to sweep away all the insects that were running riot and spreading a rotten smell throughout the mansion. I was still myself, although I understood the limits of my confrontation abilities, and knew that the outcome of the battle had already been determined. I decided to fight alongside Silwan as he confronted the mythical beasts in the Desert of Death, as though it were a battle between two civilizations, or between civilization and desolation.

It was as though Silwan had returned to that desert after breaking free of fear and had come back to help me along with Noah, who had saved him from the beasts that feared him. My God, how beautiful Silwan was. Could he hear me? "So, you've come so that we can fight the last battle together to give our dynasty a fitting ending. Let's go and confront our fate with courage, and that will be enough," I said.

On the second floor, the fat woman was getting ready to enter my private wing, but I took her by surprise. She saw the sparks of anger that my eyes shot at her, her hand froze on the doorknob, and the smile that never left her lips disappeared as fear spread across her face. I fiercely shooed her away, feeling that my entire dynasty was supporting me. My anger outpaced my footsteps, and they disappeared before me as they left the mansion's corridors. They disappeared just as they had appeared. I didn't even have to say anything to expel them.

My anger was enough to make the cowards back away from confronting me.

But I knew they would be back with treachery and bullying as their weapons. They would return like a blind high wave that would sweep away everything to death in its path. I stood still for a moment to breathe in deeply and regain my composure. They had disappeared, as had their unmistakably stinky smell.

As my feelings intensified, my silence deepened. I had learned in my childhood to swallow my words and rein in my emotions, and to wear a tight-fitting mask that did not allow any words to break loose. I was, in that respect, imitating my grandmother Mariam, who allowed nothing more than a neutral smile to appear on her pretty face, a smile that each of us could interpret differently, as each of us liked. She was hard to fathom, but her kind of mysteriousness was devoid of malice. She rarely got angry and was affectionate. She displayed strong emotions that we could sense even though she did not show them. I imitated her without understanding the degree to which she had infiltrated my depths and settled there forever. I imitated the way in which she listened to others, seeming to whoever was speaking to her as though she were all ears, although I often wondered if she was really listening of if her thoughts were in some far-off place only known to her. Her manner of silent listening was akin to humility.

Her husband liked that silence of hers and listened to it with great enjoyment. I always saw her as perfect, which was something I loved about her, and gradually grew into a copy of her, as everyone attested. Such praise pleased me, although I never knew what she was thinking.

My grandmother Mariam was the most mysterious member of the family. I started following in her footsteps as she lightly and daintily moved through the mansion, and she was everywhere. I saw in her what others hadn't been able to see. She pulled a bundle of secrets and riddles behind her, and I became an extension of her. When she died, I was perceived as the one who would take her place, and that was how I saw myself, gradually becoming both the granddaughter and the grandmother simultaneously. I behaved that way until I became the keeper of everyone's secrets, and it was therefore incumbent on me to find solutions to their problems. Everyone conspired to ensure that my grandmother's place would not remain vacant and pushed me toward it, and I happily took her place. It was from that perspective that I understood the secret of the despair that had taken hold of Balqis and Rabab and their husbands as they sensed my confusion when I told them of the arrival of the threatening bullet. They had expected me to come up with solutions, not the other way around. All those years, it hadn't occurred to any of my relatives that I might be in need of advice.

Not long after my grandmother's death, I had been able to gain their admiration, and I used it to occupy a privileged position as the heir to my grandfather's authority. My authority grew, despite my youth. I think the only one who could have competed with my status at the mansion was Julnar, but she had chosen to disappear.

My father was the happiest of them all that I had become a living memorial to his mother. The boundaries between the two of us gradually vanished, until I didn't quite know who I was.

She had passed on to me what I had considered to be her most precious and beautiful trait: her mysterious smile. It was a weapon that had given me many faces. The only place where I had managed to free myself of it, and feel that she did not want to accompany me, was the room of my lover, Father Faridoun. Could she have understood that? Had she ever had a lover?

I felt that my grandmother had played a role in choosing the paintings hanging on the walls of the large sitting room. She was someone who meditated in silence. Art cannot be understood without meditation, and meditation is not complete without silence. My choice of plastic arts as my field of study had developed my talent for silence until I had mastered all its secrets and learned how to turn it into power. The paintings became my secret keys that enabled me to pass through closed doors. The paintings absorbed me, swallowed me, fragmented my feelings and reconstructed them according to a new, more luminous concept that enabled me to experience many feelings: joy, calmness, fear, impetuousness, rapture— all shades of the spectrum of feelings that one needs to delve into the depths of existence and understand the value of life. I felt that emotions shaped my facial features, were reflected in my face and left a beautiful imprint on my soul, despite my belief that my unique features had been submerged by my grandmother's mysterious smile.

The robbers' disappearance from the mansion restored my feeling of possessing that aura. But what use would that be against those hiding in the dark? Nevertheless, their temporary disappearance was comforting, even though I knew they were nearby somewhere, biding their time.

I went out onto the veranda overlooking the garden. For a moment, everything seemed alright, at least within the limits of visibility allowed by the dust that was still obscuring the sky and seemed bent on suffocating life itself. I stared at it obtusely, overcome by powerlessness, nihilism, and futility. I wandered aimlessly from one room to the other inside the partially looted mansion, entering parts of it I had not been in for a long time.

As I left my room and went downstairs, I didn't notice that the red carpet covering the stairs had disappeared. The clattering of my shoes on the bare steps alerted me that it was no longer there. I had been focusing on the looters, not on what had been looted. Things had disappeared here and there, but that didn't surprise me. I knew that the looting process had begun. Taking stock of what had been taken was painful. Every object I could not find destroyed a part of the tapestry that was my memory, leaving ugly, holes that could not be filled. I went to the large sitting room. In my stupidity, I had feared for the seven paintings. I smiled bitterly as I shut the door behind me and saw them hanging in their usual spots on the walls. What would such people do with the paintings? It had not occurred to them to steal them. Even clothes were more important to them than Caravaggio and Max Liebermann.

I leaned my back against the reception room's closed door as I cast my confused gaze over the objects that were part of my precious memory. There were several light knocks at the door, which startled me. They were like a knife being plunged into my living flesh—because I knew the hand that carried that knife. I turned round and opened the door, and there was

Mamluka, looking into my eyes for signs of fear. I confronted her with the tranquil expression I had inherited from my grandmother, and she looked scared. It was an instinctive fear that was typical of cowardly slaves. How could a cowardly person be expected to be free? Cowardice cannot bear tranquility in its enemy's expression. This encouraged me to seize the initiative, and I asked in a commanding tone, "Have you prepared breakfast?"

Her discomfort increased, and she kept looking at me as though searching for an answer to a question she could not utter. I sensed that her expression was saying, "Wasn't our agreement that I would kill Silwan so that you could disappear?" When she was met by the expression on my face, she hurried away.

I moved around the room, looking at the paintings that had formed my early artistic sensibilities and had prompted me to study art in college. I thought about the fate of such treasures if they were to be taken by those upstarts who had barbarically destroyed the city's artistic heritage on the pretext of destroying the legacy of the regime that had tortured and uprooted them. They were incapable of understanding that what they were destroying was human heritage, or even that it might be of use to document what that regime and its predecessors had done.

I considered historical events since the heir to the throne had been dragged through the streets, unleashing a torrent of bloody violence that had escalated to the frightening extent that we were experiencing, and I realized that there was no place for the likes of us, for those who possessed the refinement and sensitivity of the artists, poets, and innovators who had been scattered to the four corners of the earth. Those who had been seduced by the dream of the democratic state we had been promised by the occupation and had been brought back by its tanks had been seized by the same nausea that I was feeling, and they could not recover.

I saw some family photographs lying on the floor. A longing overcame me to throw myself into familiar, trustworthy surroundings that would meet my need for an absent sense of reassurance, a longing for familiar faces that I could communicate with.

The ebony box studded with amber stones that my mother had brought back from her last trip to the Soviet Union was open. With a hand shaking with longing, I picked up a photograph, and ghosts from the precious past flickered before me, the living and the dead. I smelled the scent of each of them, and the scent dissipated the hatred I had felt as I watched the robbers in my mansion. Hatred disappeared. Was hatred an inborn or an acquired feeling? I laughed at the triviality of the question. The last thing I needed at that moment was to ponder a philosophical question of that nature.

It was a black-and-white photograph, taken in some home, at some time, and it felt like I had never seen it before. Or had I forgotten? Nothing was written on the back of it. It was of my father with a group of people. Who were they? Why had we never seen them all our lives? My father and the man standing next to him were the same age, in their early twenties, or slightly younger. In front of them sat two older men. My father had a friendly smile on his face.

His thick black hair was styled in a manner that gave him an air of unpolished virility. I had never seen his hair styled that way. He seemed to have abandoned that style after marrying my mother, who detested anything unrefined. There was an unusually strong look in his eyes, a hope and confidence in the future, an audaciousness wrestling with the camera lens at which he was firmly looking. His attractive eyes seemed to be saying, "What woman can resist my eyes?"

The man standing next to my father was a few centimeters shorter than him, and was smiling more warmly and calmly at the photographer. The two men who were seated were frowning. One wore traditional Baghdadi garb and looked impatient. The other, who was the eldest, frowned more severely. They were all waiting for the camera click that usually marked the exact instant when a moment that would never recur was immortalized. My father, who was younger than I was as I looked at the photo, was the most elegant and attractive.

I couldn't help thinking back on the long and painful illness that had ended with his death. My mother had refused to allow the necessary religious rituals for washing the body in the Islamic way and praying over it to be held outside the mansion, deciding instead that they should be held within it. On that sad bygone day, I had happened to go to the storeroom, where I had seen him for the last time. He was naked and lying on a low table, but it had then disappeared from my view as the men surrounding him washed his body, and a Quranic reader recited from the holy book in a beautiful voice full of sorrow, as though he had known my father personally. As soon as they saw me, they raised their hands in front of my face as though they didn't want me to see what they were doing, and their rough voices rose, commanding me to leave at once. I panicked at the sight of his thin, naked body as it underwent that ritual. Surely that wasn't my father's body. It was a very sorrowful scene. I was overcome by a feeling of alienation that remained with me even after his funeral procession left the mansion. Our faint weeping was drowned out by the sound of loud calls of "God is greater."

I had escaped into the garden's long passageway, not knowing what to do. A hand grabbed my shoulder, commanding me to follow the mourners. I complied, walking with the procession and becoming convinced that the body in the coffin was not my father, but some pale body with no will of its own, a body incapable of conforming to the image of my father that existed in my mind's eye, my elegant, charming father, whose smile had made my whole world feel secure. He had the same smile on his face in the photograph I was holding.

All our photos were hanging on the walls of the smaller sitting room. There was a photo of my father after his college graduation. He looked like a young man preparing to take on life. My mother used to say of that photo, "That is the photo that convinced me to marry him."

I picked up another photograph that had faded to a yellowish color. It was of my grandfather, Ismail Pasha, and his wife, Mariam, on their own. Their gentle smiles expressed privilege and wit, and they looked aristocratic in every sense of the word. My grandmother had left nothing to chance—how they posed for the camera, the clothes they were wearing and the choice of location and background furniture. Perhaps their long diplomatic career had taught them the skill of interacting with a photographic lens. I could never recall seeing them without the harmony that characterized them in that photograph. They seemed more like lovers than a married couple. On the wooden mantelpiece above the fireplace behind them was an hourglass with only a small amount of sand left in its upper half. Perhaps it indicated how much time they had left!

My grandparents seemed supremely elegant, but cheerless. Their gazes expressed a hauteur that seemed natural to them, two people who never allowed colorful emotions to draw close. He appeared fully prepared to turn any cheap feelings that collided with their world into pillars of salt. His moral code clearly permeated the photograph. Tears were an absolutely forbidden weakness. Displays of yearning were cheap. Love was demonstrated through action, not mawkishness; smiling was a feeling, not a meaningless stretching of the lips. We had learned that list by heart, and I remembered it nostalgically.

There was a photograph of my parents standing together with a space between them. Just as in the photograph of my grandparents, my father's right hand was on my mother's waist. There was a sliver of empty space between my parents that imparted an air of mystery to the photograph. Neither of them betrayed any sign of a smile, and my mother's mouth tilted slightly downward to one side. I knew that expression well. It was a weapon she used to express contempt, but toward whom? The dark thread of contempt across her beautiful face dominated her other features, and she seemed almost severe, as though she were performing an onerous family ritual for the benefit of future generations. But her eyes had the same brilliance that I knew and remembered. After she died and those warm eyes were absent, I felt that I had grown much older, and that her eyes had been preserving my youth.

In that picture, my father looked to be on the brink of giving us the kind of ethical lecture we had grown used to when we had behaved in a way that disturbed him or when he saw us acting with a mawkishness that did not behoove us as masters of the city. That had been one of his foremost obsessions.

I gathered up the photographs and put them back in their place, shutting the precious box as if placing an eternal seal on the past, which had become the source of a painful feeling of betrayal.

Since the resounding fall of the city of my ancestors beneath the daggers of strangers, I had felt a cold patch expanding within my internal world, growing relentlessly to include every-thing around me, my memory, my stupidities. The savageness of my alienation was intensifying under the influence of the coldness that the mysterious patch was spreading like a painful illness, a silence inhabited by unintelligible premonitions that sounded like the rumblings of an avalanche. I was witnessing the transformation of beauty in an overwhelming ugliness. My heart traveled to the places where my inherited values were piled and were being transformed into a bundle of trivia. I had been transformed into an evil force, assenting to Silwan's eternal disappearance as though he were unwanted, and not regretting it. Those who live among filth must surely become filthy, irre-spective of who they were or what category they belonged to. The elements that expose everything had overwhelmed me, and nothing could stop the deluge.

I heard a continuous knocking like the treacherous stabbings of a knife at the door of the sitting room. I waited, and Mamluka opened the door without showing her face. Her voice floated into the sitting room as she muttered almost inaudibly, "Breakfast is ready." I was familiar with her voice since childhood, but that tone of voice, which was laden with a hatred so pure that it was almost perfect, was new to me. It occurred to me that that she was hiding something else within the folds of her changed voice, but I failed to make it out. This was no longer the Mamluka that I had known since my earliest childhood, when she had never once missed calling me "*Khatouna*, young madam." Following my twelfth birthday, she had taken to calling me "*Khatoun*, madam." Strangely, by removing the feminine ending from the noun, she was acknowledging that my body had matured and I had become a woman. At the time, that made me happy because it signaled that I had joined the world of the grown-ups that I yearned for. My mother, like the other women in families like ours, had been the priestess and guardian of traditions and secrets, and she had asked Mamluka to do this. The title defined the distances and limits between those above and those below. My mother used to constantly say, "Titles protect us from others."

Ever since I had become "*Khatoun*," I had never heard Mamluka calling me by my first name, Ghosnelban, and that had continued to be the case until that moment. She decided to swallow up the word "*khatoun*" and simply referred to me by the pronoun "you," not daring to use my first name, although everything had changed, and all indications pointed to her becoming the new mistress of the villa.

Breakfast was usually served on the veranda, but the continuing dust storm prompted her to serve it in the dining room. I walked toward it, preparing myself for further surprises, which followed promptly. Mamluka had set the table for only one person. Yes, Silwan had disappeared since the previous day. Although I was aware of that painful fact, which I had contributed to shaping, the spectacle of the table laid for only one person caused a stab of pain in my intestines and I felt like vomiting. But I didn't want to do that as she watched me with great curiosity, standing by the door in an unaccustomed manner, as her looks drilled deep into me in search of tragic feelings and grief, which I managed to hide from her.

I drew on all the defiance I possessed and what I had learned from my grandmother to enable my features to resist her prying eyes. I straightened my body and could almost hear my mother's voice ordering me not to relax or show hesitation, although my back was almost buckling with grief. I walked to my chair, wearing the same mysterious smile that my grandmother Mariam had bequeathed to me, which Mamluka knew well. This was like spitting in the face of her betrayal and at all those she had brought in to partake of it. She quickly disappeared as she realized that she would not get to enjoy the sight of me collapsing. Her disappearance gave me a sense of relief.

But I knew that she would be back, that they would be back. They were biding their time and waiting in their dark places. I needed to think. The deadline was approaching more quickly than ever. The rolling hours and days could not be held back. That made it impossible for me to think. In spite of myself, my gaze was drawn to Silwan's vacant place as I waited for Guevara to come in, merrily wagging his tail.

Had I done the right thing? Was killing someone to spare him humiliation any different to killing for other reasons? I saw them all—the king, the regent, my grandfather, my grandmother, my father, my mother, and all those who had disappeared. They sat around the table and debated the question that I had posed.

They weren't looking at me. It was as if I was not there. I stood up and said, "Whatever you decide, the deed has been done." I picked up my cup of coffee and left them.

I shut the door behind me and sat facing Velázquez's painting. The dust had turned everything in the sitting room to a light-yellow color, adding a brilliant clarity to the face of the warrior god in Velázquez's painting, depicting the details of the final defeat just as the artist had painted it long ago. I stood there unabashedly studying Mars, who was powerless, in a state of semi-surrender as he awaited death with a meekness that was at odds with what we had read about him. He was semi-nude, and his battle helmet cast shadows on his face, making his features—his last remaining glory—unclear. He stared into space as though waiting for his slayer to arrive, having decided not to resist but to give in to the verdict of the council of gods, which had abandoned him. His fighting implements, which had shaped his powerful myth, were scattered on the ground in front of him, and his famous shield lay on top of them. The god of war was no longer able to fight.

I surveyed Mars's tragedy and recalled what my father used to say whenever we were in crisis. "He who sees the misfortunes of others finds it easier to bear his own misfortune." I could hear voices echoing outside the room, even though the door was closed. I knew they had returned and were taking away anything they could carry. In my mind's eye, I could see Mamluka distributing the spoils, because she knew the details and value of each piece. I wondered how long her respect for me would protect me before she would burst into the room and throw me out or hand me over as war booty to the "resistance fighter."

The mere thought was enough to make me nauseated. I realized that I had to escape. But where to? Certainly not to the homes of Balqis or Rabab. I refused to, or more accurately could not appear weak or defeated before them. I, who had arranged for Silwan to be killed to protect his dignity, had to salvage what was left of mine.

Like the whisper of an affectionate ghost amid a kingdom of destruction, Mary the cook came to mind. My heartbeat accelerated at the idea. My only choice was Mary's house. Yes, I still had the key to her house. I kept it in the box of family photos that she had left with us in trust, in the hope that one of her sons would return from abroad. She had known they would not be back, but she had hoped to keep the Christian narrative alive in its cradle. O Mary, there was a day when we had all hoped that would happen. But what maniac would now consider leaving a safe haven to return to the land of hyenas?

They key was in its place on top of the family photos. I picked it up and held it tightly, as though I were rubbing a magic lamp that I had just found. The idea of taking refuge at Mary's house after being forced out of the villa relieved me.

I was powerless to stop Mamluka and the armed men and bandits who were in league with her.

I could not understand the strong determination that was forcing me to remain in the city. Was I curious to witness its end? Or was I seeking a malicious glee in the spectacle of destruction wiping out everyone? Or was I nurturing hopes and illusions that the glories of the past could be regained? Or was I chickening out at the prospect of starting a new life far away from all the destruction? Or was I embarrassed about arriving as a refugee in cities that I had once arrived in like a princess? What bound me to a city that no longer recognized the seven generations of glory that it had given me?

I felt that I was being watched by eyes I could not see, and that I must not show any signs of weakness. I walked out with firm steps because I knew that Mamluka was watching me through one of the windows in the hope of seeing me walking in hesitant fear. I would not leave her such an image of victory. I would leave her in confusion and surprise, and even fear of me! Damn them all.

I had not left the villa since receiving the bullet with the red line around it in an ordinary envelope. It all seemed very long ago. The first thing that caught my attention on the street was the rapid and irregular movement of people. Pedestrians crossed the street, paying no heed to the cars that passed with insane speed, honking their infernal horns in all directions like curses aimed at people's heads. Their voices were loud as they exchanged words that expressed roughness and cruelty, Much of what they said included curses and cheap sexual hints aimed at emptying language of its noble human depth. Their unbearable words dropped out of their mouths like wood or heavy stones, raising challenges to my face like a glove that I was powerless to confront with anything other than contempt. They walked quickly and chaotically, wanting to get home as quickly as possible because no one felt their lives were secure on those streets of death, which had turned into an arena for the murder committed by the armed gangs that controlled life in the city and fought over the spoils of authority.

I recalled the eucalyptus trees that had lined both sides of the street. To where had they disappeared, and who had cut them down? Some children walked amid the dust, displaying their wares on cardboard boxes that they could quickly escape with in the event of an explosion or an armed fight among the gangs. They were selling Chinese-made shirts, shaving razors, cigarettes, soap, combs, sunglasses, paper tissues. One of them had a pile of bullets in front of him. He looked at me as I passed him by and gave me a sweet smile that belied the merchandise of death he was trying to sell.

The chaotic movement of cars indicated the absence of any traffic laws. Like everything else, the driving of vehicles was governed by the mood of their drivers, and they were all in agreement about honking their horns aggressively, reflecting the generally prevailing despair. The streets were crowded, mostly with men and boys. The women were wrapped in black to protect themselves from looks that threatened rape if they showed a wrist or a foot. Woe betide any woman who dared to walk the streets alone.

I walked quickly to protect myself from prying looks. I had to get there by walking down a street full of strangers. Mary's house was twenty minutes by foot from the villa. I recalled the well surrounded at its edges by pretty plants and the pomegranate, orange, and lemon trees, and Regina, who never ate lemons. I recalled the towering palm tree at the bottom of the small garden and my secret visits with my prostitute friend. I also had memories there that protected me from all the resounding absurdity that had taken hold of the violated city. Nobody would think of expelling me from Mary's house. None of her sons had returned, as I would have been the first to know if any of them had, given that I had the key in my pocket. I flirted with an evil wish that none of them would return, at least not then.

I drew close to her house, grateful that the thick dust in the air provided a barrier that separated me from everyone and protected me from their prying eyes, which tried to penetrate the dust barrier to stare at me and uproot what was left of my sense of security. Once again, I felt a sharp sense of alienation that had a burning taste.

Mary's house gradually began to emerge like a shadow. I was happy to see its green iron gate. I would content myself with the bare essentials, and shut myself in there forever. I would not even tell my sisters. They would ask me about Silwan's grave, and what could I tell them? I didn't know, I didn't want to know. Who are you to ask me?

I put my hand in my pocket and pressed the key. My hand was perspiring because of my intense emotion. Taking such a big decision was my business.

I had never expected Mary's house to be my salvation, my refuge, and my promised paradise. My memories were still scattered in its corners, I had laughed there with Regina till my tears had run. I admitted that Regina was closer to my heart, and even my soul, than all the friends I had known in my life. Regina had put me in touch with Father Faridoun, my one and only love.

Mary's house reminded me of a time when all I cared about was immersing myself in whatever enjoyment was available, a time when my mother was still alive and waiting for me to return to the villa, her eyes full of the suspicious questions that only she could frame so eloquently. She articulated them with the intelligence of a genuine Baghdadi princess, in a time when Mamluka was something other than the monster I had just left behind at the villa.

I was a few meters away from the promised paradise, preparing to throw myself into the arms of salvation when I was stopped by a woman wrapped in black from head to toe. She pulled me away to stop me from going through the green gate. I was not frightened but amazed by her behavior. When she referred to me as *khatoun* and revealed her face, I recognized her immediately. She was Regina's cousin, Hanneh. I smiled, because I had never known her to wear such clothes.

Hanneh had been a beautiful young woman, and I had been jealous of her because she always dressed in the latest fashions. Most girls were just as jealous of the freedoms that her family and wider circle allowed her to enjoy as they were of her beauty. But now she looked very different. Her face and body were covered in austere black, and very little was left of her former beauty allowing me to recognize her.

Hanneh didn't give me an opportunity to ask her about

anything and pulled me away so rudely that I almost objected. But I wanted to find out about Regina's latest news, and whether she had realized her dream of going to the top of the Eiffel tower to have a drink of arrack and enjoy the view of that bewitching city, Paris, from such a height.

"Where are you going?" she asked.

"To Mary's house," I said, pointing at it with the key that I brought out of my pocket. She continued to pull me away and said, breathless with emotion, "It's a dangerous place, don't go there."

I knew she lived in the same building that Regina had lived in. She let go of my hand and asked me to follow her so that she could explain everything to me. I allowed myself to be led by her, following her nervously. She quickly slipped through the building's gate. A middle-aged man was sitting in the entrance selling cigarettes and other items. I followed her up the stairs submissively. A sharp pain flashed through my head at the fearful thought that Mary's house was unsafe. How would I escape?

As soon as she had opened the door and made sure that she had shut it properly, she threw her black cloak onto the floor. I was standing in the middle of her sitting room, which was full of packed suitcases and others that were still open pending more things being crammed into them. I looked at her inquisitively. She looked all around her the same way that Regina used to when about to disclose a secret. The she waved her arms about, making unintelligible gestures, and said in a voice that was close to sobbing, "We're getting ready to leave."

I didn't ask her why, because the question would have been meaningless. I noted that she had used the plural, and I asked, "Who is we?"

"My son Touma and I. Most Christians have left this neighborhood. It's been taken over by armed gangs and is no longer a place for us."

"Where to?"

"To Sweden. Touma went to the green zone today to get the visas necessary for immigration."

I became aware of the terror that had started to take hold of me as I took in this surprise, and I asked, "When will you travel?"

Her eyes widened. Perhaps the stupidity of my questions had taken her by surprise. Pointing at all the things and bags scattered around the room, she said, "As soon as possible. Maybe tomorrow, if things go well."

With a terrified face, she crossed herself and said in a pleading tone, as though speaking to herself, "I ask the Lord to bring my son safely back. This city has become like a monster that swallows its children."

She crossed herself again three times, then cast a frightened and pleading look at a picture of the Virgin Mary hanging on the wall. Then she looked at me again as remembering something she had forgotten.

"Why were you going to old lady Mary's house?" she asked, as she pulled a heavy suitcase off the couch and invited me to sit down. I remained standing and said, "You know that Mary had asked me to take care of her house, and it has been some time since I went there to take a look and tend the plants that have not withered away. Since the city fell, moving around has become difficult for me, and I have been unable to come."

She surveyed me from head to toe with a kind of disdain, and said in the same sort of tone used to address a child or an idiot, "Aren't you aware of what's happening in Baghdad? The armed gangs have confiscated all the houses of Christians whose owners have left, and they are threatening those who remain every day to force them to leave so they can grab their homes. Don't you know that Mary's house has been turned into a center for one of the armed gangs?"

"When did that happen?" I asked.

She laughed bitterly and said sarcastically, "It seems like you're not from this neighborhood. It began soon after Baghdad had fallen. At first, they used to come at night, under the cover of darkness. But soon after, they took it over with all the other empty houses. First they came under the pretext of rooting out the Baath Party. Others followed, and then others."

She lowered her voice and drew closer to me as though she feared that someone might be eavesdropping, then said, "Everyone knows that they have turned it into a center or a den. They bring girls and boys they have kidnapped from their rich families and keep them there for a while. Then they either release them in exchange for a ransom or they are killed, and their bodies are secretly disposed of. At night, we hear the cries for help by the girls who are being raped. Why d'you think I am wearing these ugly clothes and this cloak? I do it so no one notices me and drags me off to that den of death."

The news stunned me. Where had I been? Why did I not know anything about what was going on around me?

Mamluka no longer gave me such news because she was part of the destructive network that had taken control of the city. So the villa and I had become legitimate targets for pillage.

Thinking aloud, I said, "So Mary's lovely house has turned into a shelter for those murderers?"

Hanneh jerked herself up angrily and faced me, saying, "I saw them myself, no one told me. I was visiting one of our relatives who left for Sweden, and I passed Mary's house. I saw a strange car parked in front of it. I had never seen anything like it. Later, people started referring to it as a Hummer. It had no license plate. Imagine, a car driving through the streets of Baghdad without a license plate. Two armed masked young men got out of it, and looked around so aggressively that all passersby lowered their heads and kept their distance. One of them then signaled with his hand, and a third person came out of the vehicle pulling out a girl who must have been in her mid-twenties. The poor thing stumbled as she tried to get her feet onto the ground, those damned cars are high, not like ordinary cars. Her dress rode up, revealing her legs. It was as though she knew what her fate would be and didn't even bother trying to cover them up or pull her dress down. She seemed semiconscious. The brute who was pulling her by the hand roughly pushed her toward the door, which someone opened. I was transfixed by the spectacle of that helpless girl. My relative, whom I was saying goodbye to, and I both cried, because we knew what that poor girl would face. You cannot image what happened after that, *khatoun*. The girl turned to us, as we were weighed down by terror, and her eyes met mine. Jesus Christ.

O Virgin Mary. I will never forget that look as long as I live. Believe me, the scene was too painful to describe. But now I don't feel sadness anymore. Sadness is a luxury for which I have no time. The only thing that I can still see in my mind's eye is the final glimpse of her as she disappeared behind the door and three armed men following her. She had given up resisting."

She put her hand over her bosom as if trying to slow down her heart rate. I thought about hugging her but I couldn't move. The surprise had floored me. Mary's house would not be my shelter. What was I to do?

I kept looking at her, waiting for her story to end, although I knew what the ending would be. A cold feeling traveled through my veins with the speed of light, a feeling of weakness and impotence as I faced the catastrophe. My God, I had actually been going to the murderers' den. What city was this? How had it been permeated by so much ugliness and cruelty?

Hanneh disappeared for a short while, returning with a glass of water and a cup of coffee, which she set before me as she looked at me with a degree of pity that I found painful. My appearance must have been bad enough to provoke her pity.

"Have a drink of water," she said.

She put her hand over mine, which was still clutching the key to Mary's house, and said tenderly as she began to understand my predicament, "The city has fallen under the control of hyenas and murderers—what is keeping you in it? I thought you would have left, like many other rich people."

I looked at her but was unable to answer her question.

The words stuck in my mouth like thorns. "I helped Regina to travel. Why haven't *you* left?" I said.

My friend's name reminded me of some of life's past sparkle. I took a sip of water and asked her about Regina.

"She's fine. She called me about a month ago and asked after you as usual. I told her you had left. I didn't know, I never imagined that you were still here. I once ran into your servant, Mamluka, and asked after you, and she told me you had all immigrated."

So that snake had been plotting our disappearance for a long time, not just since the arrival of the threatening bullet. After a long silence, she said with feminine guile, "He's still in Iraq."

I looked at her and fully understood who she was refer-ring to. It seems the question that stupidly took shape in my eyes made her laugh, and she said, "He has departed for the Nineveh plain. After the execution of the former president, we as Christians became easy prey to any upstart extremist Tom, Dick, or Harry. But I don't understand why he went north, because not many Christians are left there either, as far as I know, only some old people and a few others unable to immigrate. We are on our way to oblivion and extinction like the dinosaurs, as though we had never lived in this land for over two thousand years. We are about to disappear with-out trace. That is the way of the world—it's treacherous."

News that he was still in Iraq partly restored my sense of security. He would always be as noble as I had known him to be. Oh, how stupid I was. I still loved him and was unable to imagine any other man in my life.

The strong Arabic coffee restored some of the concentration that I had lost. I accepted the cigarette that Hanneh offered me. I was preoccupied and silent. In our situation, Hanneh and I needed to talk to calm our anxiety.

Hanneh told me what had happened to the Christians, and to many Muslims as well in the Bataween district. I heard things I never would have imagined about people that I knew, some of whom had been in college with me, and about others for whom I had felt some respect but who had turned into the leaders of gangs that murdered and robbed others.

I told her about what had happened to me, how Mamluka had betrayed me and how I had fled and come over in the hope of hiding at Mary's house. Talking was our way of reducing the pain. Once again, I recalled my father's words: "He who sees the misfortunes of others…"

Each of us expressed sympathy with the other. Her words mitigated my anger at the way I had been filthily betrayed by one of the closest people to me.

"Don't go home, I won't let you. They'll kill you and burry you in the garden. They're the kind of people who aren't held back by any ethics. Look at us. Our only crime is that we were born Christian, and we have become vulnerable to anyone willing to commit a crime. You'll stay here with me until we find a solution."

I took her hand with a feeling of real gratitude. I had no wish to go back to the villa, and I didn't think that I could. But I didn't want to burden her or anyone else, so I hesitantly responded, "No, I can't burden you like that, thanks very much."

Holding my hand and pressing it strongly, she looked into my eyes and said, almost scoldingly, "Don't you realize the danger you're in? They won't stop at taking the villa away from you. They will either kill you or force you to marry that ass who dared to presume. At any rate, under current circumstances and at this hour, you cannot return."

Suddenly we heard loud knocking at the door.

Our faces quickly changed, because knocking at the door in those times could have unexpected results. But it was her son, Touma. She yelled at him and scolded him for knocking at the door that way. But he laughed and waved the travel papers in her face with a smile of victory on his lips. Hanneh did not reciprocate his joy. She gave me a meaningful look. She had not wanted to end a two-thousand-year history in the Land of the Two Rivers by escaping, having not committed any offenses.

CHAPTER 6

HELL

HIERONYMUS BOSCH: *THE GARDEN OF EARTHLY DELIGHTS*

The dawn silence was broken by the crackle of gunfire, and the intermittent volleys soon turned into continuous shooting, and other arms were soon being used This was no surprise in the free-for-all city, but such heavy fire and the use of such weapons was unusual. Such a level of intense violence had not occurred since the city's occupation, when all guns had fallen silent.

I jumped out of bed in a panic, wondering where I was.

Suddenly, I saw Hanneh standing before me, her face displaying the same signs of panic that I was feeling. Terror made it impossible to speak. One either remained silent or screamed. We chose silence, looking at each other without so much as a morning greeting. What could we say? Good morning? We simply exchanged questioning glances, and our words dried up amid the sounds of the battle that raged outside, knowing that it could extend to where we were in Hanneh's bedroom any minute.

Our arms moved automatically with every volley of bullets or explosion, our eyes reflecting the questions in our minds, our faces full of terror, and our thoughts turning to armed gangs, the kidnapping of women, and the theft of money that had whetted the appetites of the animals fighting outside.

We only moved around slightly, glancing at the entrance of the flat, which we expected to be broken down any minute by masked gunmen firing their weapons in all directions. I couldn't understand why they were always masked. It occurred to me how trivial those face coverings were. They certainly weren't afraid of anyone, or of their victims. Perhaps they wore them to intensify our fear, we who were being robbed and violated. Or perhaps these were the everlasting traditions of murderers everywhere, traditions based on treachery. They were behind a face covering, depriving their victims of their last wish to identify their murderers.

We waited for the sounds of missiles and bullets coming at us from all directions to grow quieter and stupidly wished we would get used to them. But we realized that the situation seemed more complicated than we had first thought. We could hear military vehicles and the repulsive sound of Hummer jeeps as they drove off at an infernal speed that matched the rhythm of death that was reaping souls in the city with enjoyment for the most trivial of reasons.

Chases in the city were not between good and evil, the policeman and the thief, because it was only controlled by ranks of thieves, backed by other rows of those who waited. Since the occupation, the city was being pillaged in broad daylight before our very eyes, with each of us playing the role of thief, or accomplice, or of applauding, weeping, stunned, or frightened spectator. No one dared to try to stop the tragedy. The US occupation had taken up the coercive role that the Turkish occupation had played and that was lodged in the distant memory of a historical game of which we were the victims because we were weak. They appointed rulers that would participate with them in robbing us and keeping us quiet. They planted terrorism among us and described us all as terrorists.

A nearby explosion shook the building, which was mostly inhabited by some of the last among the last remaining members of Iraq's ancient civilizations and religions. Hanneh drew closer to me, with a look of fear on her face and a desire to weep about something she did not know. We were well aware that the door of the flat would not last long amid all those wild explosions that were shaking the place. We also knew that even if it were not blown off, it would collapse when the savages kicked it in, aiming their lethal weapons at us and shouting like animals behind their masks, yelling crude Arabic words and even cruder Americanisms. What was happening in this city, which would not stop pouring its lava over us? She came closer and held my hands, which were ice cold, and this slightly reassured me. Hanneh seemed more composed than me because she had been through a similar experience. She got me to sit down on the edge of the bed, and cautiously approached the window overlooking the street. I was terrified that she might get hit by a stray bullet and shouted at her to get away from the window. My words of warning broke the barrier of fear and cast some human warmth over the room's cold atmosphere.

She looked at me with something resembling a smile on her face, and said, "I'm trying to find out what's happening on the street below."

"Mad dogs biting one another, what do you expect?" I said.

"Perhaps it's the Americans chasing the resistance fighters," she responded.

"Here in Bataween?" I said.

"They're everywhere," she said.

"There are no resistance fighters in this city, only those who're scared."

I begged her to step away from the window and join me. She sat beside me and put her arm around me, and I felt a kind of security, pleasure, and hope. But that sense of security was violently shattered by a volley of bullets that came through the window that Hanneh had been looking through. It intensified our fear and we became hysterical. The bullets drew a semi-circle of four holes on the wall opposite the bed on which we sat clinging to each other.

She jerked me onto the floor, and we both lay there, my nose rubbing the cheap Eastern carpet. I smelled the dust and recalled Silwan. More wild volleys followed, penetrating all the building's walls and windows, reminding us of the recklessness of the absurd death that was suffocating the city. Every volley spread the same smell, and many images of Silwan, from his birth until his death. The images grew clearer until the face of Christ on the cross in the icon hanging on the wall seemed like Silwan's. The storm of bullets ruined the threadbare curtains, and the holes they made spread the smell of fires that we had become familiar with since the statue at

Firdos Square had fallen after our liberation. And now, those who wanted to liberate us again were spreading the smell of fires, mixed in with barbaric desires of destruction as they took pleasure in murder. The deafening din made me want to melt into the floor I was lying on, to turn into a meaningless pattern on a cheap, worn-out Eastern carpet, to wish for a quick death without suffering or wailing, without seeing the eyes of those firing the bullets. What was the point of clinging to life among those seeking a purposeless life, beating a path to their own deaths with a blithe stupidity?

Hanneh was unable to keep lying on the floor for long, because something else was worrying her. Touma, her son, had not made a sound. She jumped to her feet and carelessly went to the front door. She opened it, and quickly headed for the neighboring flat where her relative lived. The door to that flat was also open.

She was absent for a while, and I remained prone on the carpet, sniffing the smell of dust and dirt. I was no longer scared, because the worst that could happen was to get killed by a stray bullet. That did not scare me. It actually provided a solution to the dizzying existential questions that plagued me. I felt no desire to get up, I felt no hunger and I had no desires. I derived comfort from the feeling of being transformed into a heap of cheap flesh that drew its highest pleasure from lying on dirt and becoming totally immersed in it. The only thing I could hear was Hanneh's shouting as she spat out quick sentences in Assyrian, which I didn't understand. I felt safe with Hanneh, and I was more comfortable with her than I was at the villa.

The strange surrealism of the situation we were stuck in reminded me of a painting by Dutch artist Hieronymus Bosch. Although it depicted hell, he called it *The Garden of Earthly Delights*. It may have still not been looted and might be hanging on the silent walls of the large sitting room in the villa.

In that painting, he depicted the chaos that the Lord had threatened to visit on his rebellious servants—unbearable hell. It could only be depicted by the brilliant genius of the obsessed Dutchman, who devoted his life and exceptional talent to capturing the details of hell, which he saw in his dreams and lived with till the end of his days until they drove him insane. The creatures undergoing torture, burning humans, the instruments of hell, and its rough guards and the unending screams of those being tortured. He had painted all that in attractive colors, as though he had wanted to hide behind colors as a way of dealing with his great fear, colors that seduced one into throwing oneself into hell amid all the suffering. In the end, all he could see in the world were creatures seeking to become fuel for a great fire that all religions foretold.

Recalling that painting hanging on one of the villa's walls in all its minute details, which I knew well, restored some of my awareness of my identity, which I had begun to lose in spite of myself. Who was I? Why was I here?

The carnival of death on the city's streets had made me forget everything. I even began to feel that my presence in Hanneh's home was normal, and that the villa and the family history I had shouldered were imaginary, pertaining to a stranger I did not know.

My contact with dirt was like a pleasurable anesthetic, and even Hanneh's return to her flat slightly disturbed me, particularly since she had switched back to speaking Arabic, albeit with an attractive Assyrian accent, and she was cursing heavily. She gave me a surprised and sarcastic look, thinking that I was lying on the floor because I was scared. She did not realize the other dimension that had prompted me to meditate on Hieronymus Bosch's hell and the dirtiness of the Eastern carpet.

"Touma has gone out with his cousin to discover why the neighborhood went crazy," she said.

She crossed herself quickly three times as she glanced at the picture of Christ hanging on the wall. It had survived the wave of stray bullets. She seemed to be asking for forgiveness for his sins, which she did not disclose, as she asked the Lord to protect her son, who had fled into the street with incomprehensible recklessness.

As I stood up, shaking the dust from my dress and reclaiming my identity (Ghosnelban, the last of the city's talismans), I wondered about the reason for that torrent of bullets from all directions. Were gangs fighting each other? Or was it, as Hanneh had said, a confrontation between the resistance fighters and the occupation forces? I didn't want to get into a conversation about it, because I couldn't see the point of that. Ultimately, none of us would know anything, as usual.

Touma and some other young men from the building brought out their ridiculous light weapons and stood inside the gate to the building in the hope of guarding it against attack by strangers. Such clashes usually triggered smaller waves of robbery. There was always someone ready to rob a neighbor in the city, and everyone knew that the building was inhabited by the remnants of the ancient people of the Iraqi plain. To use the language of the rabble, it was an easy, or even legitimate target.

Every now and then, Touma came upstairs with an excited smile on his lips, like someone experiencing an adventure in a violent American film and taking on the character of a fake Hollywood hero. A look of tender satisfaction was in his eyes, and he couldn't hide his joy at the prospect of immigrating. He didn't care about the survival of his dynasty that had existed for over two thousand years. Everything had reached the brink of disappearance, and he didn't want to disappear. He was just like the sons of their neighbor Mary, who had immigrated, leaving their mother to withdraw sadly to the ancient plain where she preferred to die among the bones of her ancestors. They had left their home to the criminals, who had turned it into a den that housed their filth. "The home of Mary and Younis" no longer meant anything to their sons because they thought their future was guaranteed—or so they hoped.

I was afraid he would get killed. I tried to keep him with us as long as possible, after I caught his mother's expression, begging him to stay. I tried to convince him that it was silly to take up arms to confront militias that were armed to the teeth with America's most modern lethal weapons. But he said he didn't want to abandon his "duty" to protect us and the rest of the building's inhabitants. He remained convinced of the need to play the role of the protector and clung to his silly Hollywood role.

Man is an obedient animal. We had proven that theory. As time passed, we lost any desire to resist, or remain alert, or even be curious about what was going on outside. Hanneh would go to her kitchen every now and then to prepare Arabic coffee or food for us. But as time dragged on and we got fed up with coffee, she decided to boost the limits of our forgetfulness by offering us glasses of arrack. She brought out what was available in the fridge and offered me a glass overflowing with the magic potion. I hesitated at first, but I couldn't refuse to have a drink with the lady who had offered me protection at the most difficult of moments. I held the glass to my lips and took a sip, then put it down again, because I didn't want to become lax or careless. But I decided to improve my mood after I watched her gulp down the contents of her glass in one go, with a frown on her forehead that reminded me of Regina's when we used to drink arrack together in Mary's garden. As she watched me take another sip, Hanneh said merrily, "It's the best medicine when times get tough."

I responded to her merriment and laughter, and as time went by, I began drinking as inappropriately as I had done with another former drinking companion.

We decided to stay in the bedroom because she believed it was better fortified than the other rooms. We sat on the same carpet as I had lain on and waited for Touma. He finally joined us and told us he had managed to pick up some news about the ongoing insanity outside. Gossip and talk flew around the city with record speed, spreading like fatal illnesses in medieval times.

"They say an armed gang wearing national guard uniforms, but actually working for an important figure who controls the city, took over a bank in the al-Zawiyah district and stole millions of dollars. As the gang fled, it got into a fight with another gang that wanted its share of the booty. Many people have been killed. They say all the bank employees were killed."

I felt embarrassed by my indifference. The story didn't make me feel the slightest bit of anger. Hanneh was eating and drinking as she attentively listened to what her excited son was saying. Perhaps he was longing to participate in the fray. She looked at him proudly, smiling with satisfaction because he had brought her accurate news. Touma related the details to us in an exaggerated way, as though he were telling us about an exciting film that could only be watched in the cinemas that had burned down after the occupation. I was stuffing my mouth with food, praising Hanneh's cooking, and drinking to her health as I listened disinterestedly to his story of the massacre of the innocent bank employees.

It seemed to me as though we, as a group of humans living in that place, had descended to the level of primitive animals. We became devoid of any feeling. This was a sharp contradiction that reminded me of the frightening details in the obsessed Dutchman's painting, and I imagined it in my mind's eye. It was as though Hieronymus was saying to me, "I'm not the insane person who became fixated on hell and continued to depict it till the end. You are the ones who are insane, because you accept life in it. All I did was depict you."

My grandfather had commented long ago on the painting that was hanging on the walls of his villa. "These are our cities, and we are the torturers," he had said. Now, his message had finally arrived.

Hanneh's relative and neighbor, Muna, joined us. She and Hanneh lived as though they were one household. Hanneh told me that Muna had lost her husband in the most recent quixotic war that the defeated army had fought.

All Muna spoke about was Sweden. She had been granted humane asylum. She was still a pretty young woman, and it seemed to me as though she didn't want to live with sad memories any longer, and that her dearest wish was to exit Hieronymus Bosch's painting.

I rose from the floor, which I was not used to sitting on, with a lost smile that was mixed with a desire to cry.

They looked at me inquisitively, with questions at the tips of their tongues.

"I can now go back to the villa," I said.

Hanneh quickly got up and forced me to take two steps back, saying in an emphatic tone that was more like a command, "Impossible!"

Muna added quickly, pointing in panic toward the window with broken panes and a curtain with holes in it, "Going out now is too much of a risk, especially for a woman like you. Everything is possible. Wait till tomorrow. Please don't put us in such an embarrassing situation. We cannot take any more regret."

She exchanged that same pleading look with Hanneh, who came toward me and gently took my hand. I could not resist the tender words she whispered in my ear. She was like an angel whom I longed to embrace. She said, "We can't let you endanger yourself on the street or at that villa. How can a woman on her own go to the den of the servants who robbed her and threw her out of her villa, which they pillaged in a city that has gone insane? What do you think you're doing?"

I was resisting a strong urge to cry, which was threatening to sweep me away. My hand shook within her steady hand. She sensed my hesitation and led me to the bed, and I didn't resist. My tears flowed, and I didn't try to stop them. She had me lie on the bed, gestured to her relative to leave the room, and followed her out. Her noble gesture allowed me to cry on my own.

CHAPTER 7

MYSTERY

FRANCISCO JOSÉ DE GOYA: *WITCHES' FLIGHT*

The previous night had been unusual in every sense of the word. It was my second night at Hanneh's flat, and I knew nothing about her personal life. She never even got close to talking about it, although she was very talkative, and I didn't ask her any personal questions.

Although we had become closer at the human level, we remained in different worlds, linked by a woman we had both loved—Regina.

My night was full of short nightmares that were like razor blades sent from a faraway place. They made me wake up several times as though I had been stung, perspiring profusely and shaking with fear. I kept seeing a vague image of a woman resembling Goya's witches in his painting *Witches' Flight*. The painting had been hanging on one of the walls of the large reception room at the pillaged villa. The enchanting Spanish artist Goya had painted it during a mysterious phase, and none of those specializing in studying his immortal works had been able to understand or discover its purpose, particularly since it was part of a series of similarly mysterious and complex paintings.

As I lay on Hanneh's bed, the only thing I knew about her was that she was Regina's maternal cousin. The nightmares gave me insomnia, but I preferred to stay in bed despite my state of general anxiety and the unintelligible nightmares. I thought of waking up Hanneh. Her behavior that night had worried me. She jumped out of bed every now and then and went to the window to look at the street. But I changed my mind because, at that moment, she was fast asleep.

The only thing left to do was to drown in my thoughts about the possibilities I would have to face once Hanneh and her son and her neighbor Muna left. Those thoughts filled me with anxiety, so I tried to banish them by thinking of my loved ones, who had disappeared.

I thought of a debate I had had with my grandfather about Goya's painting, which had been one of his favorites. I thought about its intricate details, which I knew very well.

Goya had painted three witches flying in the air over a background that was as black as the devil's eye, representing nihilism and darkness. Their torsos were naked, and they wore strange hats, as though to highlight that they belonged to a very mysterious world of which we could only know fear and faith. The witches were carrying away a woman, who was trying to get away from them. Their unseen teeth were sunk into various parts of her body, which was on the brink of surrendering. A strange, pale light, reminiscent of Baghdad's dull dusty light, emanated from an unknown place, as though it were a direction no one had yet discovered. On the ground beneath the evil witches floating in the air with their victim was a donkey in a ditch. His head was lowered, he did not dare look upward, and he seemed scared.

Whenever I saw someone talking about the democracy that the occupation armies would bring us, or someone extolling the resistance against them, or someone talking about the Iraq's glories, I would recall Goya's donkey in *Witches' Flight*.

Next to the donkey in Goya's painting was a man who wore a white cover over his head and was walking toward the strange light as if determined to escape, oblivious to a man lying on the ground to his right. Each of them sought his own salvation alone. The man on the ground was covering his ears with his hands to stop the frightening noises from reaching him. He seemed to be in a state of extreme fear. Was he trying to block out the voice of the kidnapped woman who was being eaten, or whose blood was being sucked above him, or the voice of the witches rejoicing over their prey? The man escaping toward the light was the only sign of a desire to survive away from the frightening world with which Goya was threatening us.

It was past one-thirty in the morning, and I knew that the previous day had been my last at the villa, and perhaps in the city, which had been abandoned to the powers of darkness that had conquered it.

The powers of the underworld fluttered over Baghdad after the occupation had opened Pandora's box, and they were just as Goya had depicted them without knowing Baghdad or being forced to live in it.

I slept intermittently, and in between my nightmares,

I could see Hanneh making suspicious calls on her mobile phone. Whenever her phone rang, she would walk away from me as she took the call, speaking in Assyrian. She spoke in a low voice, her body language betraying confusion as she automatically glanced at me as though she were talking about me, Ghosnelban. Vague suspicions occurred to me as I vacillated between anxiety, apprehension, and indifference. It occurred to me several times to ask her about all those phone calls, but I held back the last minute. Whatever would be, would be. Mamluka had turned me over to her "thieving resistance fighter." What would Hanneh do? Would she submit me to something worse? I had discovered during that weird week that I knew nothing about the city. The only thing in my head was the history that we, the Abbasid dynasty, had built. As for its inhabitants, they amounted to something more confusing than what was depicted in Goya's painting. What could a noble woman like me do in a city taken over by the rabble, where there was no longer a place for nobleness?

Despite Hanneh's mysterious movements and my anxiety, I thought it unlikely that she would betray me. She was keen not to disturb me and to meet all my needs with a touching hospitality. The latest call she had received on her cell phone was at seven in the morning. I was aware of it because of the disturbing ring that Hanneh had chosen. It was the prelude to a song by a popular singer well-known for wailing and singing the praises of the previous regime. I considered his singing an indication of the collapse of good taste among the public.

Could all those phone calls be with acquaintances, friends, and relatives? Did Hanneh have so many of them? Sometimes her conversations with those invisible people dragged, but her expression never betrayed any annoyance, boredom, or weariness. What could take up so much talking time? But I no longer cared about the city, which was being pillaged by Goya's terrifying creatures. It was the seventh day since the arrival of the bullet.

I couldn't sleep after the mysterious session of confusing phone calls that Hanneh had made near me. Actually, I didn't want to sleep. I awaited daybreak so that I could return to the villa to capture the last details of the seven days following the threat. The details were scattered, and I tried to gather them so I could complete my narrative and understand who I was. It was as clear to me as the day, which had dawned without being marred by dust, that I had been forced into a crazy maze that seemed like a battle and that I had lost it. But it wasn't clear to me what battle it was, or why I had found myself in its midst.

The city, which had been built by our early forefathers, had never fallen easily during its long history, except with the help of the traitors multiplying within its insides like worms that consume bodies once they are buried. They had only been able to enter it after a long siege through Ibn al-Alqami's treason. His descendants had turned it over to adventurers from abroad. The shadow of the statue that had fallen in Firdos Square had not disappeared but continued to dominate the terrified city. His fall and that of those around him had not saddened me, but the city's conquest by the occupiers did. The sounds of the previous day's explosions were like that of a black prophecy.

When Hanneh noticed that I was lying awake on the bed, she went into her small kitchen, out of which she always brought nice-tasting food, and prepared breakfast. She went to her relative's flat for a few minutes, then returned, shutting the door behind her, unable to hide her restless nervousness. I asked her about Touma and she said he was still asleep, having spent the night guarding the building with his friends. I smiled at her to show my appreciation of his courage, and although we both knew that they wouldn't have been able to prevent a catastrophe had the building been attacked by the armed gangs. But their intentions had been noble.

Watching Hanneh as she ate or spoke gave me pleasure and a false sense that all was well. She came clean and told me that she did not like the idea of immigrating to Sweden but would be doing so for the sake of her son, whom she feared could become a victim for reasons she didn't know. Her disclosure about such a personal matter encouraged me to break my habit of avoiding personal questions, so I asked her about her son's father. She took a deep breath and, after swallowing a piece of bread dipped in Iraqi molasses, told me that he had worked at a shop that sold alcoholic drinks and that the "neo-advocates of virtue" had booby trapped the shop and blown it up. He had been killed instantly, as had all the other shop workers and the customers in the shop. I sensed her deep sorrow, and a tear appeared in her eye and froze. She seemed to have had enough of crying, and her smile expressed her sorrow even more.

"Nine people were killed, and we still don't know who did it. This city only registers the names of the victims, not their murderers," she said.

I lowered my head in silence. Trying to comfort her would have seemed trivial. I remained silent until she got up and began taking the breakfast things back into the kitchen. She made us some strong Arabic coffee and sat next to me, looking into my eyes in a way that signified that she wanted to talk about something more important than past events. In a low and deliberately clear voice, she said, "I've contacted him."

I felt a shiver throughout my entire body. The pronoun "him" could only mean one person. Him.

She noted my confusion and my conspiratorial silence with enjoyment, then added, "I cannot let you confront those thieves and murderers, led by that serpent, Mamluka. I never expected this of her. I cannot confront them like you do. We are too weak to do that, so I thought of contacting him for advice."

She fell silent. She knew there was no need to explain who the pronoun "him" referred to. We avoided any direct mention of his name, which was comfortable for me. She looked straight at me, trying to pick up any emotion on my part, but my face had regained an expression of neutral composure. As I remained silent, she gave up and continued, "I was able to get hold of his number in the Nineveh plain," then added proudly, "That wasn't difficult for me. To be honest, *khatoun*, you know that he isn't just anyone."

My heart pounded when she used the word "he."

She went on, "But when I mentioned you to him, he listened to me very carefully and gave me some instructions about your safety."

I remained silent, and she also kept a long silence. This time, she seemed determined that I should speak before going on any further.

In just a few moments, I discovered that I was still in love with him. At first, I smiled to reassure her and to indicate wordless gratitude.

"But…" I said.

"Don't say 'but.' He's made all the necessary contacts and told me at dawn today that your visa to Italy will be issued today and that you and I can go together to the green zone to get it stamped onto your passport."

Then she added laughingly, "That is, if Mamluka hasn't already stolen it."

I laughed as well but didn't speak. Noticing my hesitance, she continued, "Once the visa is stamped onto your passport, we can travel to Jordan together, and from there on to the wider world."

His willingness to support me gave me a much-needed feeling of confidence and the ability to think. It even gave me a feeling of joy, but that didn't last long because Silwan's ghost suddenly took strong control of me. Hanneh noticed that my smile had disappeared and asked anxiously, "What are you thinking?"

I got up and adjusted my clothes and said, "I will go to the villa."

Hanneh got up and said, "I'll go with you."

I threw her a grateful look for everything and said, "I'll go alone. This is my fate, and I am the only one who should confront those thieves."

Then I left.

The streets were calm. The people had apparently grown weary of the previous day's fighting. They walked about with a strange nonchalance. No one knew what had really happened, or how many people had been killed, or how much money had been stolen and where it had gone. I was the same. I didn't care about any of that. All I could remember was a headline about nameless employees at a bank that had been robbed.

I felt a strength and lightness akin to merriment, and an ability to confront everyone. His love would cover my head and protect me, and I would borrow the same determination that Goya had expressed in his painting in the shape of the man who seemed determined to escape the evil witches carrying off the girl, or the body of Baghdad. Could all this erase the evil that had slunk into our midst and allow love to take its place one day?

Balqis and I had once had a rare debate about things like that. She had told me that I did not make an effort to understand the people around me living with us in our city—that I was living in a bubble. She said I saw them but didn't understand them, or touch them or smell them, that they were unreal to me, that I clung to a rejection that ruled out reconciliation. Was that true? Would my knowledge of them have changed anything?

Death was in my thoughts, and I accepted it warmly. It was the only absolute that tempted me to embrace it to save myself from all the filth surrounding me. I could see it on the fronts of the buildings I was passing, the speeding cars honking their horns disagreeably, the pedestrians' clothes, the words people were uttering, and the blaring of players and radios. It was an expanding whirlwind to celebrate the bottom, powerful enough to consume all the standards of beauty in our lives. Life in such a whirlwind frightened me much more than the idea of death, which seemed attractive, even magical, offering a tempting salvation. Why hadn't damned Mamluka poisoned my dinner as well? Had she hoped to avenge herself on me and my family by humiliating me? Why all that hatred?

As I approached the corner after which the villa would be visible, my leg muscles began to fail me. For a moment, I hesitated, and a cowardly urge tempted me to return to Hanneh's flat. What I most feared was humiliation, or else, why had I killed Silwan? I leaned against a wall before deciding to press on. I had to catch my breath and calm my fear.

At last, I could see the villa, with all its doors open. My eyes quickly surveyed every part of it. It was still the same, but had lost its luster, or so I believed.

A group of children and teenagers came out through the iron gate, carrying the seven paintings above their heads and laughing. For a moment, I was dazzled by their ability to laugh as they stole. But their laughter was contagious, and I laughed as I saw them walking insolently one behind the other with the paintings over their heads as thought they were roofs that had been pulled away. I took cover as I waited for them to leave. They headed for a waiting truck, and roughly and carelessly piled the paintings on top of each other like surplus furniture, or planks of wood or old clothes that could only be used as fuel for other fires that they would light here and there as an offering to the golden calf that would take everyone to their deaths.

Max Ernst, Arnold Böcklin, Max Liebermann, Caravaggio, Velázquez, Hieronymus Bosch, and, lastly, Goya. My god. My grandparents had built up that collection of paintings, close to my grandfather's heart, over many years. It had given meaning and joy to our lives, and had given rise to questions, debates, and meditation. Here they were being thrown into a truck, which had probably been stolen as well, to head to an unknown fate, just like me, just like the city, just like its memory and history. I looked up at the sky and remembered what my father had said after the coup that had followed a previous coup. "Since the bloody coup against the royal family, our beautiful blue sky has been replaced by an angry gray sky." Perhaps he had been right. Although there had been no dust up till that moment that day, it was lurking somewhere between the angry sky and the usurped city.

Had my mother been in my place, perhaps she wouldn't have been very sad about the paintings, and perhaps about other things. She never understood my passion for the dazzling moment I experienced when looking at a painting. She had never tried to understand the secret of my joy as I thought about the moment when the artist had painted the first colored line on the canvas, unsure if he would take it to a point that would ensure his immortality or the moment when the brush fell from his hand to the floor because he could add nothing more to it. Was the artist aware of that moment from the beginning? My mother had not understood my need to dig deep into the lives of others to discover that glowing moment of bedazzlement. The poor thing, whom I missed so much, had wanted me to be a neutral and obedient member of our dynasty, which had bequeathed us the conceit that had rendered us blind enough to believe in the myth of tolerance, leading us to the brink of extinction.

Suddenly, tens of magnified voices chanting the call to prayer burst forth from the minarets simultaneously, pulling me out of the contemplation of such ramifications and the weakness that had almost paralyzed me. The only feeling that houses of prayer inspired in me was fear and much doubt. Fatwas in this city flew around like destructive volcanic lava that burned everything in its path. Everyone wanted to forget the events of the previous day, and to conceal the names of the victims forever.

Once I was sure that the thieves had departed with their spoils, I had a few remaining meters to cross to reach the villa's open gate. The first few meters separated the external gate from the internal gate, passing through the garden. Its trees were getting drier because Mamluka's husband had stopped taking care of the garden since I had received the threatening bullet. It was clear to me by then who had sent it. Had he stopped working on his wife's orders, or in anticipation of returning to the villa as its new master once I was evicted? Or maybe he didn't approve of the villainous forced robbery committed by his wife's family and wanted to distance himself? I didn't know the reason and did not want to know it, but the sight of the dried up garden and withered plants intensified my pain. That garden had been so beautiful, and my grandfather had planted its trees even before commissioning the architect Brian Cooper to build the mansion.

I walked down the pathway. We had planted our joys and fulsome memories along its edges. I could still see the shining party lights I had watched from my bedroom; I could still hear the sound of the newspaper that my father browsed over breakfast, Julnar painting her fingernails as she listened to Fairuz's songs. And there was the spot where the black crow had perched and croaked as he flew toward the Armenian cemetery, forcing my mother to visit three gilded sacred grave sites; the laughter of Silwan as a beautiful child as he ran about here and there. His body was buried somewhere around.

Men and women whose names were recorded by history irrespective of coups.

I arrived at the inner gate, which the thieves had not closed behind them. Why would they when there was nothing left to steal? They had stripped it bare, leaving it to the wind, dust, and sad memories. Evil is not interested in covering its tracks.

I could not ignore the overwhelming sense of betrayal as I surveyed the mansion's looted rooms. Its impact was so strong, it felt like it would crush me. How cruel and cheap they were. Nothing had any meaning to them. What terrible moral bankruptcy!

The looted mansion gave me an unusual sensation of cold. I had never seen it so frighteningly empty before. It seemed a lot smaller than I remembered, and I felt like a stranger, as though I had never been born or lived in it. I stood in its midst like a stranger.

Mamluka had not bothered to clean away the dust that settled on the place throughout the previous period, and it had left an awful effect that gave the false impression that the place had been deserted from way back when Ibn al-Alqami had betrayed the city to the Tartars. Something ancient, an old tale! I walked slowly from one spot to another, listening to the sound of my footsteps on the marble, which they had brought over from Italy a long time ago. I felt their ghosts surrounding me.

As I stood in my looted mansion and sensed my violated history, I was walking on the ruins left by an earthquake, and I had no idea where I would end up.

Where had all the voices stored here gone? I used to live with them, knowing that they had never departed.

Guevara…he had stopped caring about the presence of strangers among us and no longer growled at the sight of them.

Suddenly, something fluttered above me. Our dear parrot, Pavarotti, was on the loose, moving between the withered garden and the empty mansion. He recognized me and was trying to get my attention. He stood on the iron railing of the staircase to the first floor looking at me in fear and anxiety. Perhaps he was blaming me for being unable to stop the robbers from taking everything and giving him a freedom he did not want. With whatever voice I could muster, I called out to him as I used to. He was used to flying toward me and settling on my outstretched hand. But this time he paid no heed, and my voice upset him. He circled twice in the empty hallway and flew out through the open door into the wilting garden. I felt worried about him, because he couldn't defend himself against the many birds of prey coming from faraway places and flying around in the sky. They would kill him and pluck away at his beautiful white feathers. Or he would die of hunger and thirst, because he had been pampered and was unused to fending for himself. Perhaps the spirit of my grandmother, who had brought him over from Brazil, would take care of him.

The door to the large sitting room was fully open. I was not used to seeing it that way. On the floor, behind the door, lay a pile of scattered personal documents, family photographs, and my passport. The empty spaces left on the walls by the seven paintings were like eyes that were the gateways to hell. That was all that was left to me.

I went out onto the large veranda that overlooked the withered garden, trying in vain to track Pavarotti, who had probably disappeared forever. The bright sunshine reminded me of the strange light that had dominated the garden at dawn on the day of the invasion. It was of a rare quality, just like it was at that moment. It was strong, but timid. We had known that the city would collapse. All indications had pointed to that inevitability—the weak resistance, the quixotic leadership— but we had not wanted to believe it would happen. At the time, I had stood at the edge of the veranda with Silwan, a tense Guevara, and a confused Mamluka. Perhaps she had been worried about her nephew, the "resistance fighter."

We had stood there staring at the trees that were soaked by the strange light, bedazzled and anxious.

The occupation's armored vehicles snaked their way slowly along the city's arteries using their blind maps, quietly occupying one lane after the other without any noise, armies preparing to meet the unresisting, surrendering, suffocating, frightened city. Waiting to join them were middlemen, opportunists, and hypocrites, nervously preparing to pounce like hungry hyenas waiting for the lion to be sated.

What was I doing there? Did I really want to inspect all the rooms in the mansion and give them a farewell look-over?

What good would that do? The occupation and the rabble had split up my entire history as I stood by in neutrality, just like the lines that divided good from evil in this enchanting city, which feared the hyenas whose ugly savagery Silwan had described in his hallucinations.

They would be coming back. I knew that, and I didn't want to see them.